BEFORE BEAUTY

A Retelling of Beauty and the Beast

Brittany Fichter

BEFORE BEAUTY

ISBN-13: 978-1508601869
ISBN-10: 1508601860

Cover design and author profile image by Kaitlin Monroe
Cover image by Daniel Perlstein

BrittanyFichterWrites.com

To my husband, Stephen. You'll always be my knight in shining armor, my Prince Charming, and my best friend. Thank you for always believing in me and supporting my dreams, even when it means the laundry doesn't get done.

TABLE OF CONTENTS

CHAPTER 1

"My prince," a young man knelt at the entrance of Ever's tent. Ever gave him a quick glance and a nod before returning to the map that was spread out before him and his favorite general.

"Acelet, I understand what you're saying, but the plan won't work if we move out a moment before dawn. I won't give them the upper hand of the night. The whole reason we planned this for the morning was so they won't be able to use the hawks. We'll have more than enough time to send scouts ahead and split our men here." General Acelet's sharp eyes followed every move Ever's hands made on the map. Impatience was in the general's face when he finally jerked his chin at the disheveled figure still waiting in the corner of the tent.

"You're one of the king's men, aren't you? What are you doing here?"

"Prince Everard, your father bade me to deliver this!" For the first time, Ever looked directly at the man who thrust a sealed, water stained parchment at him. His voice shook and his clothes were tattered. Something must have gone very wrong. His father had been adamant that their regiments not communicate between campaigns.

"Where is Corbin? Why did the king send you instead?" The young man could have been no older than seventeen. His thin shoulders shook as he spoke, though whether from fear or being soaked by his rainy trek, Ever couldn't tell.

"Corbin is dead, Sire. I barely made it out before they took the camp completely."

"Dead?" General Acelet stared at him in disbelief. "That man has been the king's favorite messenger for twenty years." He frowned at the skinny boy. "I find it hard to believe that the enemy could get close enough to kill one of the king's favorites." The young man paled and glanced at Ever. Seeing that he was expected to speak, he went on, his voice still trembling.

"The king's campaign was unsuccessful. We took too long to reach the valley, and it was nightfall by the time we arrived. Princess Nevina was upon us before we could set up the defenses. Her men burned our supply wagons on the first night, and the hawks have kept us trapped in our own tents ever since. Not that they needed the monsters," his eyes clouded. "The darkness the princess sends over us is . . . too much." He finally looked straight at Ever. "Your father says he cannot master it." Fury rippled through the prince. All thoughts of the map aside, he strode over to the trembling young man and grabbed him by the shirt.

"I don't know what game you think you're playing," he snarled, "but no matter who has bought your allegiance, you will regret blaspheming my father's name with such insults of weakness."

"Sire!" The young man desperately pointed to the letter still in the prince's other hand. "I beg you, read the letter! I cannot read, but the king spoke the words as he wrote them. I heard as I waited in his tent!" Ever glared at him a moment longer before dropping him at Acelet's feet. When he finally held the wax seal up to the candlelight, he could see that the seal was still unbroken, so the young man could not possibly have read it. A wolf with jewel shaped eyes stood over the corpse of a serpent, baring its teeth and crouching for another pounce. An uncomfortable voice in his head wondered if the messenger might be telling the truth, but he dismissed the thought before it was complete. Breaking the seal, he read what his father had hastily written.

"Everard, our campaign has failed. Their hawks have multiplied greatly since our last encounter. Whether through informant or traitor, they knew the location of our first encampment, and were upon us before the first night had passed. We lost many men to the hawks and even more to the arrows they rained upon us in the dark. The siege would have been manageable if their arrows had not burned our supplies, also. Their worst weapon, however, has been the dreams. More men have gone mad with each passing night from the visions of confusion and blackness that the abominable princess sends. And those who avoid sleep grow mad with exhaustion. I am finding my own thoughts difficult to follow as I fight the darkness. It is with shame that I admit I cannot match her power. We cannot wait until tomorrow. You must come now."

For the first time since he had become a man, Ever felt a cold shiver of fear run down his back, despite the misty heat of the spring rain. His father had never been as powerful as Ever was, but he'd never been rendered helpless in battle. Was he completely unable to protect anyone but himself? Numbly, the prince read the letter again. He could feel Acelet's eyes on his face, keenly measuring his reaction.

"What does the king say, Your Grace?" Ever straightened his shoulders and cleared his face of all emotion.

"Nevina has apparently gathered numbers greater than we had anticipated," he answered carefully.

"Will we be moving out earlier then?" Ever took a deep breath before shaking his head.

"No. I will not give her the advantage of the night the way my father did. I can protect us here, but not in the mountain passes. We'll move in the morning as we planned." Acelet bowed his head in acknowledgment and excused himself to finish making arrangements, taking the unfortunate messenger with him. Ever returned to the bench and looked at the map again. As he traced the paths his men would take the next morning, his mind drifted back to the days of planning he'd spent with his father. He couldn't understand what had gone wrong. They'd been so careful.

"I don't want Nevina close to the Fortress. She knows too much," King Rodrigue had stated before they'd even discussed any strategies. "I want to cut her off in the desert valley just north of the border. If my men and I wait in the valley before she arrives, you can bring your men through the mountains to close in on her from the east side."

"How do we know when she plans to attack?" Ever had wondered.

"Acelet has sent spies, but he believes it will be within two weeks. If we leave soon, we should be prepared to strike by the time she reaches the valley. Even if she guesses that we'll cut her off, she will expect to see our forces coming from the south, directly from the Fortress.

"You'll wait here," his father had pointed to a crevice on the backside of the mountain. "Instead of coming from the south, you'll be poised to pour down from the east." Ever nodded. He knew the place well. There were large caves there that would shield the men from view, should Nevina send her hawks in for a closer look. The large caverns would allow him not only to hide two hundred men from Nevina's spying eyes, but they were close enough together for him to shield his men's minds from her visions as well.

"I'll send a runner to the valley to let you know when we've arrived," Ever had begun, but his father was already shaking his head.

"No messengers. No communications of any sort. You may be able to shield your men in the caves, but you cannot be expected to do it for travelers as well. I will be too busy to look for messengers. Without our protection, the runner could easily be discovered. Nevina would have the information out of him in minutes."

His father had been so confident in their plans. And he had every reason to be. King Rodrigue had never lost a battle. Small skirmishes happened often with some of the border lords, but few kings were foolhardy enough to challenge Rodrigue directly. With the strength of the Fortress and the harsh determination of its monarchs, Destin's borders had not been breached in over two hundred years. Most of the king's great battles had been fought coming to the aid of their allies in neighboring lands.

Ever's father had followed in the footsteps of his fathers, and it had served him well. King Rodrigue had known nothing but the study of warfare since boyhood under the watchful eye of his own father. When they drew plans up against Nevina, there had been no bravado in the king's schemes, nor had there been a false confidence. The preparation had been as straightforward and focused as his plans always were.

And yet, as they'd strategized in the king's study, Ever hadn't been able to ignore the waning light in his father's eyes. The glowing rings of blue fire had been growing dimmer for years, but Ever had lacked both the courage and the heart to bring it to his father's attention. It would have drawn both shame and outrage to question the Fortress's power that resided within him. Besides, the Fortress wouldn't allow his father to falter in the midst of his greatest battle. Ever had been sure of it.

But now, here on the mountain as that battle raged, Ever felt the fear stir within him as he reread the lines his father had written. The Fortress had indeed allowed his father's power to weaken, enough for him to call for help in a way he never had before, enough for his men to die horrible deaths of fear and fire as the king cowered in his bed, hoping his son would save him. Every weakness Rodrigue had ever despised, he had assumed in sending that letter.

In his weakness, Ever decided, his father must have succumbed to the shadowy deceptions of his enemy. Those suggestions of hopelessness and confusion must have galled him into sending the messenger. And Ever knew that when his father was once again in his right mind, he would look back on Ever's decisions now and judge them as harshly as he ever had. Ever had been right in telling Acelet to stick to the plan. Besides, it didn't matter if things were as dire as his father described. His men would not survive the night outside the caves. They would have to wait until dawn.

The next day, everything went as planned. The sun was bright and hot, and as soon as its rays touched the mountain paths, Ever's men fanned out. They crouched along the rocky paths, awaiting Ever's signal to move. Ever lay down on a ledge that jutted out over the valley and crawled toward the edge to get a better view. It seemed the situation had gone from bad to worse since the messenger had been sent. Throughout his father's camp, the yellow Tumen banner fluttered brazenly over the tents. Those of his father's men that he could see were sitting cross-legged on the ground, chained to one another and watched by large guards. Not only had Nevina attacked his father, but she had beaten him soundly. It was alarming how quickly her strange band of ragtag vagabonds had grown into an army of hundreds.

Still, from the arrangement of her regiments, it was clear that Nevina expected him to come from the south. Ever breathed a sigh of relief as he realized he still had the upper hand. The dark princess might have many men, but her powers were limited. As terrifying as they were, most of Nevina's monstrous hawks could not stand to fly by day, and her men's arrows did not shoot as straight without the dark of night to guide them. Without the winged scouts to circle the skies, the enemy wouldn't see Ever's men until it was too late. Satisfied, Ever gave Acelet the nod. The general, in turn, motioned to his archers to begin the assault.

Their arrows filled the morning sky, sending the enemy scrambling as Ever's footmen began to descend upon the camp. The prince poured his strength into his men as they moved. He could feel Nevina attempting to fill their minds with visions, but she could not penetrate the shield he had created around them. Her rogue forces were caught off guard as Ever's men surrounded them. In just minutes, his father's men were freed, and the valley once again belonged to Soudain.

Most of the enemy had fled in fear by the time Ever followed his men down into the valley. He surveyed the carnage and was somewhat surprised at how little blood had been shed. None of his own men had been lost, although he had no idea what kind of damage had been inflicted upon his father's men before he'd arrived. The same couldn't be said for Nevina. Although it seemed that the princess had escaped unscathed, her numbers were devastated. Acelet had the captives that remained rounded up and executed on the spot.

And yet, in spite of the enormous victory, Ever's stomach churned as he strode to the king's tent. King Rodrigue tossed and turned in his makeshift bed, moaning. Beads of sweat ran down his white temples. His appearance was so shockingly altered that even the healer hesitated before walking to his side. The arms that had been hard as rock when the king had left the Fortress were now thin and shaking. The king's face was haggard, and his features emaciated. When he turned to look into Ever's eyes, he looked not like the most feared king in the region, but a frightened old man.

Ever immediately ordered everyone out. The healer grumbled, but Ever still sent him away. The prince couldn't understand how the king had lost all of his strength to Nevina's power so quickly, but he could see that the blue fire in his father's eyes was nearly extinguished. This was something only the power of the Fortress could heal, and the only two persons with that strength were staring at one another from across the room.

Ever needed to work fast. Pulling his gloves off, he knelt by his father's side. Taking his father's hand, he clutched it tightly in both of his. Closing his eyes, he focused on the dim light his father was still clinging to. He caught his breath as the enemy's power bit back at him. He hadn't known his father could suffer the power of evil like this. The princess's darkness had indeed grown. The desire to tremble filled him greatly, but he could not give in. He tried with all his might to reignite the fire in his father's eyes, but every time he pushed, it flickered dangerously.

"Son," Rodrigue rasped. Ever opened his eyes to see his father staring at the wineskin of water on his small bedside table.

"Father, I need to draw her power out. I need you to help me." Ever felt as if he were talking to a child. His father shook his head, however, looking again at the water. Frowning, Ever let go of his hand and gave him the water instead. After the king drank, he whispered,

"Why didn't you come?" The look that passed through Rodrigue's eyes pierced Ever to the heart. Was his father actually blaming him?

"You know I couldn't have protected my men in the pass at night. If we had tried, my men would have been in the same position as yours." His words were as close to a rebuke as he had ever dared to give his father, but the frustration that welled up in him was nearly more than Ever could take. After thinking for a moment, the king nodded heavily and laid his head back down. Ever picked up his hand again, but the king withdrew it.

"Everard, my mistake was not arriving too late, as you might think. My mistakes have been years in the making. My eyes are dimming. I know you've noticed. I've left my people unprotected. I could see it in the Chiens' eyes when Nevina took the camp." He grabbed Ever's shirt and pulled himself up, suddenly glaring at his son through leaden eyes.

"The Fortress has chosen a new king, one that will be a better king than I. But it will reject you, too, if you ignore the cry of our people. You must protect them!" Exhausted, he fell back into the bed. Ever tried once again to take his hand, but the king whispered, "Just let me go, Son. The spirit of the Fortress will carry me to my fathers, and I will rest with them. It's your turn now." And with those words, the king was gone. In a dirty tent with one candle to light the room, the great warrior king had admitted defeat and left his son to pick up the pieces.

"Your Highness," Acelet knelt at the doorway of the tent. "The grief of the kingdom is with you." Ever swallowed hard and finally stood, still staring at his father's body.

"How are the survivors?"

"Not well, Sire. I'm afraid I must ask you to go to them. Many have gone mad from the dreams. There's nothing else I can do for them." With a nod, Ever turned sharply and left his father's body. He had work to do, and he was suddenly grateful for the princess's poison. The work of healing would occupy his mind for now. Deep down, however, he knew he would have to mourn sooner or later. For all the monsters he could slay, for all the darkness he could pierce with his light, for all the unearthly strength that he possessed, he did not know how to mourn. And it terrified him.

. . .

The king was properly lamented by the kingdom, but Ever had an uneasy feeling that it was more out of respect than true affection. Although the Fortress courtiers and servants wore black and offered him all the right words in the wake of his father's death, he often heard them speaking excitedly of his upcoming coronation when they thought he couldn't hear. This irritated him more and more as the week drew to a close.

"Shall I tell them you wish to be left alone until the midday meal?" Garin calmly gestured to the manservants present that they could leave. Ever put his head in his hands and took a deep breath before answering. Although his annoyance at one of his barons still lingered, he sought to control himself. His father had taught him not to share too much with his servants, but Ever had never quite been able to sever the connection he had with the Fortress steward. During the early years when he was still too young to be of much use to his father, Garin had been there. And he needed him now more than ever before. The prince sighed.

"I'm supposed to meet with the Duke of Sud Colline in an hour," he wearily told his steward. The duke was prudish and had been since they were boys. If Ever was too blunt, his distant cousin was just as likely to speak for an hour without actually getting to his point. Garin put his hand on Ever's shoulder and spoke softly.

"I don't think it would be too much to ask that your subjects give you time to mourn. It's only been five days, and the funeral is tonight." Ever groaned, and Garin walked to the door. "I'll speak to your cousin. If he is not satisfied with my words, then he shall simply have to remain unsatisfied." Ever couldn't help the small smile that escaped his lips. Garin smiled back and bowed before leaving the prince alone. Unfortunately, while the silence allowed him to elude his courtiers, it made it even harder for him to avoid his own thoughts.

The sensation settled upon him quickly as he wandered over to the balcony that overlooked the mountain. He'd heard others wonder at the terrace's purpose, as it showed nothing of the kingdom or its boundaries, but it was one of his favorite spots in the Fortress. It faced the peak of the mountain, just higher than the slope the Fortress was built upon, rather than the valley and its city that spread out below. It gave him the illusion of solitude more than any of the other windows in the citadel. The lush green tree line abruptly ended below the bare summit. During the warm months the summit was covered in nothing but dirt, but in the winter it was covered in crisp, clean snow.

He closed his eyes and imagined how the snow would feel now. He'd hiked there once as a child. Though it was still considered part of the Fortress grounds, no one went that high. He'd been young, only nine, too young to venture out on his own, but old enough to know better. Still, he recalled how the snow had felt as he buried his bare hands in it, how quickly they'd numbed. If only he could feel that numbness now. If only he could shove his heart in the snow and leave it there. It didn't matter what he desired, however, as the guilt was going nowhere fast. His father had always lectured him that guilt was pointless.

"It forces you to look inward," he'd growled once when he'd caught Ever apologizing to a servant. "It leaves you open, susceptible to attack by others. When you are focused inward, you're distracted. A distracted king is a king begging for enemies to show their faces." And Ever had tried. He'd learned over the years how to ignore the feelings that welled up within him. It was hard, as it is for any child born with strong affections as he had been. But he'd trained himself to push those feelings away, to lock them up by focusing on what needed to be done. And yet, this guilt he couldn't push away.

It's not fair, he thought to himself as he turned back to prepare for the funeral. He'd gone over every detail, every scenario in his head. He'd searched for any way he possibly could have saved his father. But each scenario he'd imagined still ended the same way. He'd listened to his father's instructions down to the letter, and in the end, he knew he'd made the right decision to wait. He simply could not have protected his men in the night. They would have all suffered the same fate as his father and his men. And yet, that did not erase the guilt that now coursed through his veins and made his face run hot and his eyes moisten at the corners.

The funeral was perfect down to the last detail, thanks to Garin. The tapestries had been drawn, shutting out the light of the fainting sun. Candles lit the huge hall only enough to see the casket at the head of the room. The black coffin had been polished so well that Ever could see his dim reflection in its sides as he approached it. His father lay there in his military robes, a gold braid draped across his chest. In his hands he held a scepter carved out of chestnut wood with a small crystal at its tip. The royal priest uttered words of tribute to King Rodrigue, describing to the kneeling mourners the king's great feats and his daring victories, but all Ever could focus on was his father's face. It was stern now, as it always had been, except for the night of his death. Then, it had been full of fright. Just like the girl's had been.

Ever nearly took a step backward when her face flashed before his eyes. He had tried his best to push her away, but her midnight blue eyes, wide with terror, had followed him in his dreams every night since his father's death. It was all her fault.

He'd never had a reason to feel great guilt before she'd stumbled, literally, into his path. He felt his anger burn suddenly as he struggled to keep up with the priest's words. He was sure the guilt over his father's death would have been easier to push aside if it hadn't also been for the lingering guilt brought by the nameless peasant who haunted the dreams of her prince.

Ever had been thirteen when it happened. The day had started out beautifully. It was the morning of the Spring Holy Day, and he was out exploring the Fortress's lands, as usual, before it was time to watch the annual procession. He remembered it so well because he'd nearly fallen out of a tree from shock when his father suddenly appeared in the clearing below him.

"Everard," Rodrigue had called. "I can feel you're near. I want to speak with you." Ever knew it must be something of great importance. His father never fetched him personally. He always sent a servant instead. If it had been a servant calling him, Ever might have dropped out of the branches right in front of him for fun, but he knew pranking his father would end badly. He climbed down instead.

"Yes, Father?"

"Ah. Garin said you'd be here. I want you to return to your chambers and prepare for the procession." Ever knew better than to question his father, but he was confused. The procession was still two hours away. As if Ever had spoken his thoughts, his father answered them. "This year you will be riding in the procession with me." As they began to walk back toward the Fortress, Ever had turned and looked up at his father in wonder. He'd never been allowed to hold a place in any of the capitol processions.

"You are old enough," King Rodrigue continued, "to be seen as a leader. When you take the throne one day, I want them to be confident in your strength and ability to protect them. If we begin showing them now that you are indeed serious about your duty, they will accept you readily, even hungrily when I am gone."

"Yes, Father."

"Before we leave, there are expectations you must know about, duties that if you neglect them today or any other time, could be disastrous to your future rule. Do you understand?" He'd turned a gray eye and glared down at Ever through the blue rings of fire, and Ever had nodded ruefully. He had a feeling he wouldn't like these rules.

"First, you must remember that you are to be present with the people, but you are above them. And that includes the servants. You are not to speak with them unless giving an order. While I wish you would adopt these habits in court, the way I've been telling you to for years, you *cannot* forget them in public. You know our strength makes us responsible for these people. We must protect them from our enemies at all costs, but to be vigilant we must be removed. You cannot be scanning the horizon for spies, so to speak, when you are giving your attention to one or two peasants in particular. Distraction makes us vulnerable."

"Will we be looking for spies during the procession, Father?"

"We are always looking for spies. You are no longer a child, Everard, and today is the day I expect you to begin acting like a man. Now go to your chambers and the tailor should have your clothes ready. You will meet your mother for the procession when you're finished. I will be there soon after."

Ever had done as he was told. When he arrived on the Fortress steps, his mother was already on her horse. He bowed to her, and she gave him a small smile and nod before turning to instruct one of her ladies-in-waiting about the smelling salts she needed to forget the stench of her mount.

The procession was grander in person than Ever had imagined. He'd only ever seen it from balcony windows. His horse was stationed between his father and mother's horses. All around them, tall flags with the royal wolf seal were raised up high on green velvet squares edged with gold braided trim. The procession always began at the Fortress, moving down the mountainside and into Soudain. Once in the town, it snaked through prominent streets before returning back up the mountain in a giant loop.

Since the monarchs were always at the end of the procession, the first performers would be returning to the Fortress before the royals even left. His father's best soldiers were scattered in groups of six throughout the performers, and more were stationed along the procession path. They wore no bright colors. Gaudy men had never been of any use in battle, his father always said. They were too easy for the enemy to see. Instead of wearing the Fortress colors of blue, green, and white, his father's men simply had the image of the wolf impressed upon their chest plates in black silver, burned into the metal by the finest artisan blacksmiths in all of Destin.

Ever had to remind himself to look regal. He'd never been allowed to visit the capitol city before. Soudain was too full of distractions to be good for a prince, his father had always said. Until now. Now the streets glowed with the brilliant orange of the setting sun, and flames lit the tops of the lampposts that stood on every corner. Families crowded one another on the edge of the streets to wave to their rulers. They always bowed low before his father, and Ever couldn't help but notice that their smiles nearly disappeared when he turned to glance in their directions. Fear, he decided, was the overarching emotion they wore. To Ever they remained bowed, but he noticed many of them dared a peek at their prince. A number of them, particularly the girls, gambled a smile. He would nod and turn back to the street, hoping his actions were as his father expected.

As his horse rounded a corner, a movement in the crowd caught his eye. A few boys were pushing to get to a better spot in line. One of them shoved too hard, and a girl who was standing at the edge of the crowd was knocked right into the street. Without thinking, Ever hopped off his horse and bent down to help her up. She was lanky with auburn hair and large midnight eyes. Her dress was simple, but neat and tidy, which meant her family probably belonged to the skilled worker class.

As soon as his hand touched hers, he felt his face redden with shame, and he could feel his father's icy glare on his back. So much for staying removed from the crowd. Helping the girl stand, he nodded quickly at her and turned to get back on his horse. His father would have some choice words for him later. He didn't dare look at the king. The procession had come to a halt as the people watched the actions of their young prince with a sudden pride, but none of their opinions mattered. He had failed his father.

Eager to be on his way and ready to forget the whole ordeal, Ever was nearly on his horse when he felt a tug on his sleeve and a gasp from the crowd. Turning, he saw the girl had lost her bewildered expression of shock, and had followed him to his horse, and even dared to do what his servants did not.

"Thank you, Your Highness," she looked up at him with eager eyes. Anger pulsed through him. Why couldn't she just let him alone? Impatient to be rid of her, he roughly pushed her hand off his arm. As he often did, however, Ever forgot the amount of strength that ebbed through him. What he'd meant as a simple brush shot blue fire from his arm to hers. She fell backward, right in front of a cart horse. The horse startled and reared, and with two sickening cracks, landed on the girl's wrist and ankle. Ever watched in horror. She screamed as the villagers rushed to her side.

"Everard!" His father's voice was sharper than he'd ever heard it. Slowly, he tore his gaze away from the mess he'd made to look at the king. "On your horse!" The fury in his words was unmistakable, and Ever miserably nodded and did his best to finish the procession. But as he rode, he could hold his head high no longer, and every time he closed his eyes, the look of pain on the child's face was there before him. To make things even worse, Ever's father was not kind that evening after the celebration was over.

"Not only did you deliberately disobey me, but you made the situation worse with that wretched temper of yours! Now we have one more cripple to live on the streets and beg, one more unproductive citizen to waste precious resources on!" Ever doubted she would live on the streets, judging by the clothes she was wearing, not that his father would ever notice that kind of thing. But his father was right. He'd added one more helpless, unproductive citizen to his kingdom, one more thread of weakness for the enemy to target. His mother said little about the incident, except to complain that the pause in the procession had been bad for her hair. Garin and Gigi were the only ones who seemed to understand how he felt.

"And is the young prince wanting some hot cider tonight?" Garin had slipped in that evening, as he often did when his duties were done. Despite the enormous load of work that King Rodrigue placed on the steward, he always seemed to have time for Ever. That night, however, not even Garin could cheer him up. The boy had shaken his head as he stared sullenly into the fire.

"Come now, Your Highness," Gigi, the Fortress's head kitchen matron slipped in from behind Garin. Despite his protests, she set a cup of steaming cider down beside his bed, and proceeded to adjust the pillows around the boy. "Tomorrow will be a better day." She smiled gently at him from underneath her mop of silver curls. She patted his cheek affectionately with a soft hand before wishing him goodnight, leaving him alone with Garin. Garin walked around the room straightening chairs as Ever sipped his drink. The only sounds were the crackle of the fire and the scrape of furniture against the floor.

"I did something bad today," Ever finally spoke, his voice cracking twice. Instead of denying it, as all of the courtiers had done, however, Garin spoke with painful honesty.

"I heard about that. How badly do you think she was injured?"

"It looked pretty bad," Ever admitted. Garin just nodded. He waited a few moments before speaking, and Ever found himself strangely anxious to hear what the older man would say. Disappointing his father had been bad enough. He didn't know if he could bear to have the steward disappointed in him as well.

"We all make mistakes, Sire. Some, unfortunately, cannot be mended as easily as others. I have found, in my humble experience, that when we hold positions of power, our mistakes often hurt more than just ourselves. They hurt others. It is something we must live with." He was quiet for a moment before adding, "But the important thing is that we learn from our mistakes. What you did today was indeed unkind. But you will be no better off if you simply regret it. You must learn from it so that you never hurt another like that again. Everyone makes mistakes, Ever, but a true leader takes the knowledge he gains with him, and he applies it toward his future.

"Now," Garin gave Ever a smile, his eyes crinkling kindly in an expression very different from the one the king had worn when they'd parted. "It's time for you to sleep. Like Gigi says, tomorrow will be a new day." Ever had hoped their kind words would make sleep easier, but the moment he shut his eyes, he saw the look of hurt and betrayal in those dark eyes again.

The incident took longer to forget than he'd hoped, but eventually, with the help of his father, he learned to shut it out, along with any other distractions that bothered him or might steal his attention from defense of the kingdom. For that was his duty, his father said.

"Other kings live in soulless buildings, cold and austere, castles that provide little motivation for defense other than their own personal comforts. But this place, our Fortress," he ran his hand lovingly over the marble walls as they walked. "This Fortress is the source of our strength. It is what sets us apart from others of our rank. It must be protected at all costs, and its kingdom as well. There is no other like it, and there never will be again. And it knows," he had turned a sharp eye to his son, "when we lose our focus. Keep your eyes on the horizon, Everard. You never know who might be coming to steal that focus and this Fortress from you."

It hadn't been an easy road. Ever's father, always able to focus on the horizon, was like a statue with eyes that never wavered, or even closed for that matter. Ever didn't have that kind of vision, the ability to block out all but the goal. Instead, he was inclined to notice the slight changes in seasons, or when a servant was acting differently because of an illness or suffering.

From a young age, he'd loved exploring the Fortress grounds. He found a peace, a quiet communion of the soul with the colossal citadel when he was deep in its sheltering greenery or underneath its stone arches. It took great effort for him to throw off the childhood desire to pause sometimes and simply exist in the secret places of his beloved home. It was somewhat painful to treat the servants like people other than his friends, particularly those who had been just that during his solitary childhood years. And yet, his father said, it was what he must do in order to protect it all from the destructive forces of those who would destroy such a paradise.

Little by little, under Rodrigue's guidance, Ever gained the ability to focus as his father did. His strength, which had been unusual since he was a small child, was honed, and by the time he was a young man, he'd been wrought into the warrior prince not even his father could have dreamed of. The girl's face had faded into little more than a bad memory by the time he was twenty-six years old. She only surfaced when he was tempted to feel guilt, which thanks to his father, wasn't often. She had reappeared, however, the night his mother died.

Ever had been out riding his horse, training with some of the archers, when a distant figure waved him down from a great distance. As he approached, Ever could see Garin's thin frame, and something in his stomach had turned uneasily. While he'd obeyed his father and cut sociable ties with most of the servants, he'd not been able to tear himself from Garin. Out of respect for his father, they didn't flaunt their communication, however. If the steward was coming out to find him personally, something had to be wrong.

"Your Highness," Garin had bowed in his saddle as he rode up to the men. "I think you might want to call today's practice short. I have . . . a message for you." Dismissing his men, Ever guided his horse over to walk beside Garin's. The older man's graying hair was messy, as if he'd pulled it back in a hurry, and his clothes, for once, were rumpled. "Your Highness . . . Ever," he finally turned to the prince. "I'm afraid I am not quite obeying your father's order, but I thought you should know before he called you."

Ever gawked at the steward. While Garin often stretched boundaries and rules, he had never disobeyed King Rodrigue outright. "Your mother has died," Garin continued in a quiet voice. "You know she hasn't felt well in weeks, and today she slipped away from us while she slept. Your father wanted me to wait until he could tell everyone, but I thought you should at least have time . . . ." His voice faded, but Ever nodded unhappily. As much as Ever had become his father's protégé, he still was unable to completely block feelings like Rodrigue. Garin had known he would need time to think before he was called before the entire court to hear the news.

Garin had gone after that and left Ever time to be alone before the courtiers were gathered for the official announcement. He struggled to pin down a name for the emotions that flooded him. That there were emotions was undeniable, and none of his father's training could banish them. Many feelings swirled around in his mind as he thought. Strangely, what bothered him most, he finally decided, was that he was not sad.

Ever had spent years watching his servants interact with their families, and as a young child, had even interacted with them when his father wasn't looking. The parents would call, and the children would respond with shrieks of delight, running to their parents for hugs and kisses. It had never been so with his family. His father had shown him affection in his own way throughout the years by preparing him to be the best king he knew how. Queen Louise, however, had never seemed to feel the maternal affection he saw in the servants and even the mothers of noble blood. Ever and the queen were amiable, and greeted one another always with respect and kindness, but there was never anything more. Guilt, he realized, was the emotion that ran through him. He felt guilty because he recognized very quickly that her death did not bring him pain. He would have felt more pain if Gigi had died.

On the night of his mother's death, the girl's face had visited him in his sleep for the first time in years. The pain in her eyes and her look of utter heartbreak broke his heart. He might have been able to ignore her in his wakeful hours, but at night, he was hers.

He wasn't yet completely recovered from the queen's death when his father had announced that it was time for him to pick a bride. All the eligible women and girls of proper status and bloodlines from the surrounding kingdoms were invited, and within a week, they had arrived at the steps of the Fortress, each aspiring to be the next princess of the most powerful kingdom in the land. Ever had watched them descend from their great coaches, each girl glittering more brightly than the one before her, decked with diamonds and pearls and silks.

"You look as if someone has just handed you a prison sentence," Garin had teased him while they prepared.

"Any chance my father will rely on the Fortress tradition to choose one?" Ever had asked glumly. Garin's smile vanished, and he shook his head.

"I doubt it. As much as your father loves the Fortress, there hasn't been a queen chosen the old way in three generations. Your father will be evaluating the political strengths of each union, rather than the girl herself." Ever could only nod. He'd suspected as much.

His mother had been a duchess from a neighboring country, and her marriage to his father had joined their armies as allies. It was a wise political match, to be sure. Still, Ever was decidedly against having the same relationship with his wife as King Rodrigue had fostered with his mother, one of polite greetings and farewells in passing. And yet, it seemed an unavoidable fate. Within an hour, he was presented to the court and was obligated to begin dancing.

The weather was fair, and the moon shined brightly on the balcony on which dozens of couples twirled in time alongside him. Fortunately for Ever, though there were many, many girls, he was a good dancer, and making conversation was easy for him. Beautiful faces and lovely smiles surrounded him, and sweet greetings and giggles filled his ears, blending together despite his attempts to remember which princess or noble lady belonged to which land. He'd had no idea as to how he would choose one, but as always, he worked to honor his father's wishes. His confusion aside, the evening was fairing tolerably until he suddenly found himself face-to-face with a woman he more than recognized.

Princess Nevina was indeed a beauty, but not in the typical sense. Nothing about her was delicate. Her dress, made of black, silky feathers sewn together tightly with gold threads, was cut low to reveal her generous proportions. Her arms were also bare, and boasted sturdy muscles, not large, but rock solid. Her hair was dark like her dress, and her eyes were a surprising green against her bronze skin. Every move she made was lithe, and her eyes glowed brightly as she looked Ever up and down shrewdly before accepting the hand he'd automatically extended.

"Everard," her low voice was smooth. "It's been a while since we've met on such amiable terms. I think in our separation you might have outgrown your father.

"Perhaps so," Ever's voice sounded strange in his own ears, tight. He had not expected the Tumenian princess to be among the invited guests that night. As they began the dance, he dared an accusatory glance at Garin, who shook his head ever so slightly. That meant his father had invited her. Had he lost his mind?

The princess of Tumen and the prince of Soudain had not last parted on pleasant terms. Introduced as young children, as most of the royal children were at this ball or that tournament, they had gotten to know one another well enough. Nevina was unlike the other children, however, in that the moment Ever laid eyes on her, he'd realized she had a deep strength akin to his own. But where Ever's strength had always been one of light and life, the young princess's power was heavy, nearly sickening. She seemed to be aware of her effect on him, too, as she'd smiled when Ever had to ask Garin to accompany him back to his chambers early, away from the tournament festivities.

He'd been seven at that first meeting. As they got older, not only did he train himself to resist her powers, but to even mute them as well. They didn't see each other often, as Tumen's continuous push for influence among the surrounding nations strained its relationship with Soudain. It wasn't until they were eleven that the two young royals met again, and much to Nevina's outrage, not only did Ever stop her attempts to torment him, he'd stopped her attempts at tormenting anyone else at the gathering as well.

Their encounters had been sporadic over the next ten years. When he was a young man, diplomats had begun to report that Tumen had given up its ambitious goals, and desired nothing more than peace, but Ever was skeptical. Even *if* her father was seeking to give up his ancestors' dark power in order to obtain peaceful relations, Ever never doubted for a moment that the princess had every intention of keeping and using those powers to boost Tumen's strength, with or without her father's blessing. Only recently, her schemes had been interrupted by an unexpected arrival.

"Come now, Prince," Nevina gave a little laugh, jolting him out of memories and back to the present. "Let bygones be bygones. Our kingdoms have grown beyond their conflicts, have they not?"

"I certainly hope so," Ever responded curtly. He doubted it, however, as he watched the gold fire dance around her green eyes.

"Then dance with me as you would a woman who might actually deserve you," she drew herself closer to him. Ever's heart beat even faster as he tried to keep a chivalrous distance between them, looking desperately for his father over her shoulder as they turned.

"I hear things have changed in Tumen," Ever tried conversing again, desperate to keep her from continually pressing her body against his. It was distracting, and he could see people beginning to notice. Court gossip was inevitable, but this was one tryst he did *not* want gossiped about.

"If you're speaking of the birth of my brother, then yes." Her eyes tightened just enough for him to see the gold fire roar in spite of her calm appearance.

"I'm sure there are many men desirous of your hand." Ever's voice was polite, but Nevina didn't miss his words' significance. "You have much to offer."

"Pray tell then," the princess purred. "Why exactly am I here?"

"Sire," A small voice interrupted their spin. Sending up a prayer of thanks, Ever stopped dancing and released the princess so he could turn and talk to the boy who suddenly stood beside them. It was inappropriate behavior for a servant, but the boy was young, and Ever was grateful for the break in the conversation. Before he could appropriately reprimand the boy, however, Nevina had reached down and slapped him across the cheek. Ever couldn't keep the indignation from his face as he turned to look at her.

"You dare touch my servant?" His voice carried loudly, and for once, he didn't care. The music stopped as everyone watched.

"Prince Everard!" She gaped back. "His impertinence was an insult to me and my kingdom. If anyone should be apologizing, it should be you. In my country, our servants know their place!"

"I don't care how you abuse your useless Chiens! My people are in the service of the Fortress, and you will not touch them!"

"So this is the strength you boast of, you who are revered far and wide." Her voice was suddenly cool and quiet, and somehow, even more unnerving. "And yet, you do not have enough control over your own to allow you a single dance with me. Your Fortress is weakening, Everard Perrin Auguste Fortier." Her mouth had curved up in a strange smile, and her eyes were nearly closed as she spoke. He realized suddenly that she had been waiting for this, the opportunity to test and push him. She wanted his kingdom and was searching for any chance to challenge him for it. This revelation infuriated him even more.

"Get out of my home. Leave my kingdom, and do not return," Ever growled.

"Oh, we will be leaving," Nevina's captain of the guard was suddenly at her side, glaring at him. Nevina's golden flames blazed even more brightly as he spoke. "We cannot, however, allow this insult to our sovereign to go unchallenged."

"Soon," Nevina's voice was a purr once again, "as you watch your men fall, Everard, remember who it was that caused the bloodshed. Know it was your own weakness and cowardice that was your undoing." Ever gritted his teeth as she then waved her hand dismissively. "Let's take our leave of this place, Captain. We'll be back soon enough." With that they turned, Nevina's skinny Chien girl hobbling along behind them as quickly as she could.

And that was where it had all begun. Within an hour, the guests had been dismissed, none of them announced as his bride. For that, Ever was grateful, but he had little time to revel. He was immediately called to his father's study. It was there that they chose spies, ran through battle scenarios, and had agreed to break the army into two camps, one on the mountain and one in the valley. It was on that eve that King Rodrigue had insisted they have no communication between the camps before they engaged their enemy from the north.

"Father, there is one thing I don't understand," Ever had hesitated before returning to his chambers when they were through. "Why was she even invited? Was I supposed to ask for her hand in marriage?" His father had sighed.

"It was a foolish hope on my part. Our relations have been better these past few years. I believed we could forge a union between our powers that would prevent future wars of this sort."

"But their power is not like ours," Ever frowned. "It's one of deception and darkness. The Fortress would not abide that sort of queen."

"Everard," his father had fixed his gaze on him in a strange way. "I'll be honest with you. Where I once felt the strength of the Fortress run through my blood, there is emptiness now. I do not feel its direction anymore. It's up to us now more than ever to protect our home in these strange times." It had been on that night that Ever had noticed the extreme dullness of the fire in his father's eyes, the slight trembling of his arms and hands. And yet, he'd remained silent.

Now he was dead. And as Ever stared into the casket in which his father lay, he could see nothing but the face of the girl.

CHAPTER 2

"Find Solomon for me," Garin instructed one of the servant girls as she ran by him. As far as any guest was concerned, the coronation ceremony was going splendidly. The aromas of the seven course feast were wafting out of the kitchens, filling the halls with the smells of wild boar, aged cheeses, and spiced stews. Candles lit every corner of the Fortress, making it as bright as day. Wine flowed freely, making the guests even merrier as they awaited the coronation of their beloved prince. Unfortunately, Garin had a feeling the guests weren't the only ones enjoying the drinks tonight.

He wound his way through the guests as he quietly searched for Ever. It shouldn't be so hard to locate the man who was an hour away from being crowned king. Garin was thankful that none of the guests seemed to suspect anything. Even before they had begun to partake in the drinks, their faces had been alight with the hopes and dreams that rested on Ever's shoulders. King Rodrigue had been a good king by most standards, and Garin had sworn his loyalty to him without question, just as he had done with Rodrigue's father and his father before him. But Everard was different. Even those who knew little of the incredible power that flowed through the prince knew he was special.

Ever had always been different. Though his father had missed the prince's birth, as he'd been off on a campaign against one of the border lords, Garin had been there. The queen's labor had been difficult and long. Garin had done his best to keep the Fortress servants productive, though it was difficult with Louise's screams echoing down the stone halls.

There was a strange sensation in the air, one of anticipation. The Fortress hadn't felt like this on the day of Rodrigue's birth. Garin had not felt anything like this in a long, long time.

"What are you up to?" he'd muttered to the Fortress as he made his way to the queen's chambers, squeezing between the serving girls as they ran to and fro bringing clean blankets and whatever else the midwife ordered. There had been no words in response, only an even stronger tugging at his heart, one that bid him to walk more quickly. As soon as he stood outside her door, the screaming stopped. A baby began to cry, and Garin strained to hear what the midwife was saying. Seconds later, a chambermaid scurried out, nearly running right into him.

"Begging your pardon," she curtsied. "But I was just sent to find you. They think you should see this." Garin entered the room, the privacy curtains now closing the queen off from his view. The midwife had already expertly cleaned the child, and was swaddling him as Garin approached. No words needed to be said. Garin nearly gasped as he drew closer.

Inside each of the child's eyes was a bright ring of blue fire against the gray irises, encircling the pupil. No child had ever been born with the strength of the Fortress so evident, not like this. What made it even more surprising was the weak fire Ever's father, grandfather, and great-grandfather had all held. The queen had no fire at all. Garin knew immediately that this child had a purpose, one that the Fortress hadn't given to a king in generations. He also knew it was his job to help the boy find it, for his father, as passionate as he was, would be too blinded by his own agenda to value what truly set the child apart.

In the week after Rodrigue's death, Garin's fears had been rekindled, his concern that the king's myopic focus would have disastrous consequences in one as powerful and sensitive to the world as Ever. With each day that the prince came closer to being crowned the king he was meant to be, he'd seemed closer to losing himself. Each day he'd trained harder and eaten less than the one before, and each night he had sleep terrors that made him cry out and wake in a cold sweat. Each night, he had called out about the girl.

Garin wasn't the only one concerned for the prince. The other servants, though less familiar with the ways of the Fortress than he, had become increasingly unnerved by the prince's erratic behavior as well. And when the prince could not be found an hour before his coronation, Garin had a sick feeling in his stomach that it was going to all come crashing down that night.

"You sent for me, sir?" Solomon came hurrying up to the steward.

"Yes, I did. Do you know where the prince is?" The man grimaced a bit.

"Forgive me, sir, but I'm not supposed to tell you." Ah, so Ever was going to play that game, was he? Garin huffed impatiently.

"Well then, why don't you tell me where he *isn't*?" Solomon relaxed a bit. Glancing up at the king's study, he said quietly,

"The prince is *not* in his chambers or with his guests." He paused before adding, "He is also *not* drinking *wine*." Garin sighed and nodded as he headed up one of the spiraling staircases, away from the bustle of the grand entrance, where guests were still being received.

"Your Highness," he cracked the ornate wooden door. "You've never had more than a few glasses of wine. Are you sure this is a good evening to begin something stronger?" Opening the door further, he saw Ever out on the small balcony that overlooked the back lawn. Ever was slumped against the door frame. His powerful shoulders were hunched over as he spoke.

"The crowds made it too hard to think." His words were slightly slurred.

"Yes, they often do that," Garin agreed cautiously as he joined the prince on the balcony. Ever's face was twisted into an emotion that tugged at the steward's heart. Despite the savior Prince Everard had become to many, defeating the dark forces of the north, Ever, the young prince was still there underneath, and he was grieving.

"But the quiet is even worse. Still," Ever finally stood and walked back to his father's desk. "I have finally figured it out. I understand why Nevina led her men to attack. I understand why my father died. And it wasn't my fault!" He suddenly slammed his hand down on the desk with a bang.

"You're right, it wasn't your fault."

"It was their fault!"

"Their fault?" An uneasy feeling stirred in Garin's heart.

"Call my advisers, Garin," Ever ordered, taking another swig from the flask in his left hand. "I'm going to stop these threats once and for all!"

"Sire, it's the night of your coronation. Surely this can wait until tomorrow," Garin suggested hopefully.

"No, it cannot. My father always said our enemies would be waiting, and he was right. We must cut them off *now*!" With a sigh, the steward did as Ever demanded. It didn't take long for all of the prince's advisers to gather in the king's study.

"You all know my father believed the strength of the Fortress was our great secret in defending our land," he began, his words still slightly blended. His advisers exchanged wary looks. "He taught me to look for weaknesses in our lines, to search for the chinks in the armor of our great armies. After much thought, I've realized that the lack of strength in our armies wasn't what allowed the enemy to inflict such vicious casualties."

"Your Highness," General Acelet stepped forward cautiously. "The darkness in our enemy's power was one we hadn't anticipated." But Ever waved him off.

"Just hear what I have to say. Our chink wasn't in the strength of our men, but in the weaknesses of our people. We have too long coddled the unproductive citizens, the weak that inhabit the streets of our cities and live off the hard work of others."

"Sire," Garin gently reminded him. "They haven't lived off the grain of the Fortress in years. Your father cut off assistance to the churches years ago."

"It doesn't matter!" Ever turned to his steward and jabbed a finger at him. "If we did not have these beggars, these diseased and lame lying in our streets and in our churches, Nevina never would have dared to attack us. There wouldn't have been a weakness to pursue! And I've decided it will never happen again!" As Ever uttered his next words, Garin felt sick. "I command that our land be purged of its weakness. You will all go out and make sure those who cannot contribute to our strength are no longer a threat to Destin's well-being."

"Your Majesty," General Acelet's face was white and his voice quivered. "You can't be suggesting we kill our sick and crippled!"

"That is exactly what I'm saying, General!" Ever bellowed. "You are to begin tonight, after the coronation." He strode unevenly up to his favorite general and leaned his face so close to the man their noses nearly touched. "And if you don't have the manhood to carry out my orders, then I'll have to find someone else who will."

"Please, Your Highness," Dagin, the horse master, pleaded. "It is late, and the ceremony is about to begin. Please allow us to wait until the morning to reconsider and discuss this again."

"If one more soul questions my order, then he will find the same fate as the diseased that will be soon cleared from the streets," Ever barked. "Now, it's time for my coronation. Garin?" Nodding blankly, Garin struggled to quickly help Ever into his ceremonial robes, which had been haphazardly tossed over a chair earlier. The other men each bowed to the prince in turn, their faces pale and full of fear. They hurried off as quickly as possible, leaving Garin to his charge.

Garin searched desperately for something, anything that might change the prince's mind, but from the look on Ever's face, there was much drink left in his body, and addressing him would only make him angrier. So Garin kept quiet, but that didn't mean he would sit idly by as Ever stained his hands with innocent blood. If Garin could not prevent all of it, perhaps he could put off some.

As soon as the prince was dressed, Garin excused himself. Running back to his chambers, he whipped parchment and a quill from his desk. The ink smeared as he wrote in haste, but the words were legible. He gestured to the first servant he saw.

"Give this to Edgar. Tell him to take it to Ansel Marchand in Soudain. And tell Edgar that if he values his position here at the Fortress, there must be no delay. That goes for you, too! Now hurry!" As soon as his message was dispatched, Garin tried to regain control of himself. In all his years at the Fortress, he'd never felt such a sense of dread wash over him. The prince who had always been the Fortress's favored one, more than any other king, was quickly bringing something evil upon them all.

What can I do to stop this? He begged the Fortress silently as he walked quickly back to the throne room, where the ceremony was beginning. As he took his place in the back, he noticed many of the other advisers returning as well, from similar errands he was sure.

Ever had somehow managed to get himself down the aisle and before the priest without rousing much suspicion from the guests. Now, as he stood before him, laying his hand on the Holy Writ, Garin felt a pang of sorrow. This should have been an eve of joy, not one of murderous bloodshed. The kingdom had waited for its beloved prince, its jewel to become their sovereign since the day he was born.

Before the prince could utter the ceremonial vows, however, the priest abruptly withdrew the Holy Writ and took a step backward. Uneasy murmurs spread over the crowd as the old man's face pulled into a frown and his eyes became engulfed completely with blue flame.

"Everard, son of Rodrigue, son of Damien the Fourth, the Fortress has declared you unfit to wear this crown." A gasp went up from the assembly. "From the day of your birth, you were gifted with a strength unknown to other men. Because of your callousness, however, what has never been done before will take place tonight."

The old man raised his head and turned his fire-laden eyes upon the ceiling. "The Fortress will go dark, and you, Prince Everard, will be a prisoner of your own making. Before life can be found in this sacred place once again, a new strength must be found. What has been broken must be remade. The one who was strong must be willing to die. Only then can the Fortress and the kingdom have the protector they deserve."

As the priest finished speaking, a dreadful grinding sound filled the hall. Garin fell to his knees, trying desperately to block the noise as the lights began to go out, one by one. The world around him seemed to rise, and rushing winds burst through the great doors, and as it swept through the people, each one began to disappear. Then all was silent, and there was no light.

CHAPTER 3

"Your eyes are sparkling," Deline smiled at her daughter. Isa beamed back.

"It's perfect." And it was. The dress was simple, but it was everything she could have hoped for. The gauzy white made her feel like she was floating in a cloud. Her arms were covered in lace, and her veil made the world look like the clouds filled the room. Best of all, the long gown covered all but the toes of her shoes. If she stood still and buried her hand in the layers of white material, it was impossible to see the crook of her ankle or how her left wrist turned inward.

"No, Baby," her mother wiped a tear from her eye. "You're perfect." Isa fought the tears that threatened to spill down her own face. She still couldn't believe this happiness was hers. At one time, she'd thought it never would be.

It was hard to imagine that just months ago, she'd been running for her life. After receiving a midnight letter from a friend at the Fortress, Isa's father had dragged the family out of bed, whispering severely that there were to be no candles or fires lit. Deline had wept as Isa's father and brother had bundled her up and buried her beneath a load of supplies in the horse cart and fled the city in the dark of night. For three days, they had waited up in a deserted mountain cottage before Deline had been able to send word that Isa would be safe again. The Fortress had gone dark, and the royal order had never been carried out.

Still, when they had returned, the neighbors said Ansel should send his daughter with the Caregivers. It had been a close call. While years had passed since the Fortress monarchs had shown true interest in the welfare of its poor, everyone had hoped their new king would bring about a more merciful reign. Instead, Isa had very nearly been killed in her sleep by the first edict of the young prince. No one knew when the Fortress would awaken, the neighbors said, and then what would become of Isa? No, her father had argued, much to Isa's relief. Isa was staying with them.

It wasn't that Isa disliked the Caregivers. They seemed kind enough. Merchants by trade, they would come with great varieties of foreign wares, many which her father sold in his mercantile. They didn't just trade for money, however. Everyone knew the Caregivers by the black metal rings they wore. Those rings, they claimed, were a sign of asylum for anyone who needed sanctuary. Unbeknownst to the king and his elite, those who could not provide for themselves were smuggled out with the Caregivers to their own country, where they were given fitting jobs, food, and shelter.

This was all fine and good, but it had always bothered Isa that those who left were not allowed to contact their families. It was too dangerous, Marko said. Marko was one of the Caregivers who visited Soudain most. An old family friend, Ansel often purchased his goods for the mercantile. Marko was a good-natured man, and since they were small children, he had never come to the mercantile without sweets for Isa and her brother and sister. He was fiercely built for a tradesman, and would have frightened her if she hadn't known him for so long. His long hair was always pulled back into a tight knot at the back of his head, and he smelled of campfire smoke. Marko had visited not long after the Fortress went dark, and he had strongly advised Ansel and Deline to send Isa with him as well.

"It's too dangerous to leave her here!" He'd argued, gesturing in the direction of the Fortress with one of his large arms.

"I will not send my daughter off by herself to a place I have never been and will likely never see," Ansel had answered his friend in a steady voice.

"You could come with her! We would happily take you back with us, all of you!"

"It would be too conspicuous," her father had shaken his head. "I'm on Soudain's city council. They would notice when I left. No, I will care for my daughter. She will be safe with her family."

That had been the end of that discussion, even when other acquaintances and friends had urged Ansel to send her away, and Isa was grateful. After a few weeks, the Fortress had remained dark, and the urgings had stopped. Life began to return to normal. Well, better than normal for Isa. Raoul had asked her to marry him.

Isa smiled to herself as her mother repinned her dress one more time. Tonight, everything would change. Tonight, Raoul would return from his journey with his father, and she would become the wife of the future chancellor. She imagined, as she often had in the last months, what it would feel like to see him again. They'd exchanged letters, she more than he, several times since he'd gone. His father kept him busy with political meetings and social events, so his letters were far and few between, but such was the life of a chancellor. She was fine with that. It was simply a pleasure to write to him, something most women wouldn't have been able to do. But tonight, she would have no need for quill or paper. This would be the night she would wed the one who had been able to see past her brokenness.

"Now, we have no time for crying," Deline wiped both her face and her daughter's. "The guests will be here soon, and I can already hear your aunt ordering everyone around. I will be back up when it's time." Isa watched as her mother left, and felt a familiar pang. She would miss her mother. Most women would have been nearly beside themselves with worry, trying desperately to get their grown daughters married, particularly if they were Isa's age and still unwed. But not Deline.

"You'll always have a home here," Deline had told Isa the day she got engaged. "No matter how old you are or how many years pass, you can always come home." With those words in mind, Isa carefully practiced the wedding dance steps as she waited impatiently. She had decided to forgo her sturdy walking boots in favor of the beautiful white slippers her father had commissioned the tailor to make for her. They would make dancing more difficult, but she was determined not to give anyone a reason to smirk or whisper. She would be as beautiful and graceful as any bride this night.

"Isa," Deline finally opened the door. "He's here. It's time." Taking a shaky breath, Isa tested her ankle once more before beginning down the stairs. It seemed like the whole city was there, crowded into her parents' home. Friends, neighbors, and family smiled at her as she slowly descended, but they weren't the ones she was looking for. There. Her groom stood by the door next to his father. Straight backed, he held his head high. His brown coat was clean, despite having just returned from a long journey, and his black boots shined. Slicked back with oil, his neatly trimmed hair matched his boots. What she was most interested in, however, were his eyes. Dark brown, nearly black they were so dark, they reflected the light of the dying sun as sunset passed through the shuttered room. And they were looking right back at her.

As soon as she saw him, she remembered just how handsome he was, why all the other girls had been so jealous when he proposed to her. That a crippled girl should have the son of the chancellor was unthinkable. She who couldn't walk evenly didn't deserve the responsibilities of being his wife. And yet, he had chosen her. Isa walked as carefully as she could, making sure not to teeter in front of the crowd, until she was finally standing before him.

His dark eyes were wide and his face was taut, as though he was afraid. She shared the feeling.

Cautiously, she curtsied.

"My lord," she uttered the first words of ceremony, just as she'd been practicing for months. "May my life strength be bound to yours."

"Isabelle," he whispered, "we need to talk. Alone." Isa stared back at him, momentarily unsure of what to say or do. Not only had he failed to give the ceremonial response, but he'd called her Isabelle. He hadn't called her Isabelle since they were children. Something, she quickly realized, was very wrong. Nodding slightly, she began to tremble as she turned to walk to the back door of the house. Whispers and gasps went up as they walked. In addition to all her other woes, Isa miserably admitted to herself that wearing the silken slippers had been a bad idea as she struggled toward the door. After a few slow steps, Raoul stiffly offered her his arm. Silently, everyone watched them leave.

Isa's mind was spinning. They should have begun the ceremonial dance by now. She felt as if she were stepping out of one of her daydreams and into a nightmare. As they sat on the garden's low stone wall, she realized she didn't want to hear what he had to say.

"Isabelle, we've been apart for some time now," Raoul began slowly, his gentle voice strained. Isa nodded silently, staring at him with fear knocking her heart about in her chest.

"You know my father took me along so I would learn how other chancellors and governors lived. He says that living here can sometimes blind us to the traditions people of our station must carry on. It's too easy to get wrapped up in what we desire for ourselves, and what we truly need in order to best serve the people." Isa nodded again. She had known this, as he'd written about it in one of his first letters.

"We saw many other administrators while we were gone. Eight, actually. Some lived like lords, and others had little more than their people. But they all had had one thing in common." Raoul dropped his eyes the ground. He didn't go on. It took Isa a moment to realize he was talking about her.

"Their wives," she quietly whispered. Raoul nodded. It was a moment before Isa was could speak. "So, you're saying I'm unfit to be a chancellor's wife."

"Now wait–" he began to correct her, but she held her hand up angrily.

"I can read and write, which is more than you can say for many men in this wretched town. I can figure the sums of the treasury better than you can! How is that an unsuitable match for a chancellor? What more could you possibly want?"

"I need a woman who could rule in my stead if something happened!"

"No! No, what you mean is you want a mindless ninny who can stand by your side without having to lean on you for support! A flawless flirt who can charm visiting politicians with her grace and allure! You want a woman without a crooked hand or a lame foot!"

"Belle–"

"Don't call me that!" She was shouting now. "Just tell me one thing. Was this your idea or your father's?" He stared at her for a long moment before softly saying,

"It was my father's wish for me to see how others lived, but it was my choice to live like them. I want what's best for this people."

"Then take what you want and go." Isa's father was suddenly beside him. "But before you do, I want you to know that neither you nor your father are ever welcome in my mercantile or my house ever again." Ansel wore a look of deep hatred Isa had never seen before. "Men without honor have no place in my home."

With a weak nod, Raoul looked silently down at her hand. Isa realized what he wanted, and angry tears spilled down her face as she yanked the ring off her hand and shoved it at him. No words seemed to come to the young man as he stared down at the silver band, so after a long moment, he simply turned and walked out the back gate. Isa and her father sat in silence for an immeasurable amount of time before she was finally brave enough to speak.

"Is everyone still inside?"

"No, your mother cleared them out after I asked Chancellor Dupont what his son was up to." Isa nodded, and before she knew it, her father had drawn her close and held her tightly. She could hold back no more, and before long, she realized she was wailing. She'd felt pain before, like the day the prince had shoved her into the way of the rearing horse. She'd felt grief when she'd realized she could no longer dance. She'd felt sorrow when the other children left her alone to find more suitable play spots, places she could not walk to or climb.

But Raoul had always been the one to tell her it was alright, to stay with her when the others had run off. He had been the one to ask her to dance at all the town festivals when no other young men dared to. Raoul had been the one to nickname her Belle. He had been the one who believed she was worth marrying, despite her handicaps. But he had lied. And none of the pain she'd ever known compared to this.

Isa cried into her father's shirt until she could no longer sit up straight. It wasn't until she was tucked into her own bed that she realized she'd dozed off. She was still in her white dress, but she didn't bother getting up to change. Instead, she lay in bed and listened to her parents in the next room over.

"Did he say *why*?" Her mother asked.

"Some nonsense about how it was acceptable for his son to befriend a crippled girl, and even ask her to go dancing sometimes." Ansel's voice was low, but Isa could hear the dishes they were collecting clatter and bang a lot louder than necessary. “But as Raoul’s father, it was his responsibility to direct him toward important matters, now that he’s a man. He didn’t say as much, but I can tell you right now that Isa’s the reason he took him on the trip, to show him what a chancellor’s wife *ought* to be.” At that moment, a dish shattered and Ansel cursed. Isa’s parents were silent for a long time before Deline spoke again.

“I’m worried about her, Ansel. I’ve never seen her like that.” Isa’s father gave a loud sigh, and Isa could imagine him running his hand through his graying hair.

“Me, too. But she’s a strong girl. She’ll get through it. She has to.”

Dawn was slow to come the next morning. Isa had drifted in and out of a tearful slumber. The light, however, brought little relief. Finally, Megane got out of her bed and crawled in with Isa. Isa held her little sister tightly, which released another set of tears. Megane watched her anxiously, but was silent until it was time to get dressed.

“You should fold that nicely,” she said as Isa crumpled the wedding dress and threw it in the drawer. “Then it won’t be wrinkled for the next time.”

“There won’t be a next time, Megs.”

“Why not?”

“Because men don’t want crippled women for their wives,” Isa spat out the words before she remember whom she was talking to. Megane’s eyes grew wide and she hurried out of the room. Isa felt badly for speaking to her sister in such a way, but she couldn’t chase the bitter words from her mouth.

As she collapsed back onto the bed, she felt her anger grow. Not just for Raoul, but for all the girls who had told her cripples don’t get husbands. For all those people who stared at her sympathetically every time she walked the city streets. For all the women who had nudged and winked at her as the wedding day had approached. For her small bed that should have been empty last night. But most of all, for the prince.

If it hadn't been for him, she never would have been a cripple. She would have continued to dance, to run, and to grow and laugh with the other children. She would have been called beautiful by more than Raoul as she became a woman. She would have known the touch of a loving husband by now. It didn't matter that no one had seen the prince since the Fortress had gone dark. Isa suddenly hated the man with a vengeance she didn't know herself capable of until that instant.

The day didn't improve things any for the family. After they spent all day cleaning up what should have been a wedding feast, Ansel came home from the city council meeting with grim news.

"The chancellor wants someone to visit the other cities and towns to see if their tradesmen have suffered as we have since the Fortress went dark."

"And let me guess," Deline sighed. "He chose you."

"He's just angry that you stood up to him last night!" Isa's younger brother, Launce, muttered into his stew.

"I believe you're right," Ansel said to his son, "but whether he's angry or not makes no difference. The other council members agreed to it. I leave tomorrow."

"How long will you be gone, Papa?" Megane asked.

"Quite a while, Sweetheart," Ansel lifted his youngest daughter out of her chair and into his lap.

"You're not going all the way to the western hills are you?" Deline frowned. "Surely they wouldn't make you go that far!"

"Unfortunately, yes. I'll probably be gone until the leaves change color. But don't worry," he kissed his wife. "I promise to try and be back before the first snow."

So Ansel left the next morning with all his provisions in saddle bags on one of the family horses. Goodbyes were tearful, all except the one he exchanged with Isa. Isa felt as if there were no more tears left to shed in the whole world. The rest of the family watched as he made his way east toward the mountain pass, but Isa turned and went back inside. Looking at the pass meant seeing the Fortress as it rose up out of the mountain side. And looking at the Fortress meant looking toward Prince Everard.

CHAPTER 4

Ansel wrapped his cloak around himself even tighter as he started down the mountain. His journey had taken even long than he'd thought, and the eve of his return looked like it might be have to be postponed. The black clouds above him were heavy with snow, and he still had a long descent ahead of him. Even in good weather it would have taken him two hours to make it down to Soudain, but the biting wind whistled eerily as if to promise it would take him much longer than that.

The trip had not been encouraging. The other cities and towns Ansel had visited were also suffering. Trade and travel had slowed to a crawl after the Fortress went dark. Without the protection of the Fortress and its kings, fear had driven many of the smaller towns to close their borders, and those that had remained open saw few tradesmen or merchants. Ansel would be forever grateful that the darkening of the Fortress had spared his daughter's life, but he now hoped that he had enough in his own mercantile to feed his family, much less those who came to purchase food throughout the winter.

Another large gust of wind interrupted Ansel's thoughts, and when he looked up, he realized white flurries were already beginning to descend. Within moments, it was nearly impossible to see the road. He quickly considered what he should do. There were no mountain cottages this high up the mountain that he could seek shelter in. In fact, the only thing that he could possibly reach before the blizzard fully struck would be the Fortress. And the Fortress was dark.

More icy mountain air hit him as he considered this. After the Fortress had closed, the townspeople had whispered to one another of curses and all other sorts of dark magic. Ansel had paid little attention to it, simply thankful that whatever had happened had kept Isa alive. Besides, he was a practical man. He didn't have the time to sit around fretting about gossip borne of daydreams. Now that he was suddenly faced with the choice of visiting the great Fortress, however, Ansel had to admit that he felt a bit of unease. Even if there was nothing to the rumors, his family's last run-in with the prince had turned out to be more than disastrous.

Still, he reasoned, he had no choice. No matter how he felt about the prince, he had friends there among the servants. Surely when they saw who was knocking upon their doors, they would be willing to open up and provide him simple respite in their quarters until the storm passed. The prince need not even know.

It wasn't long before Ansel was able to make out the post that marked the way to the servants' entrance. He coaxed his tired animal onto the dirt path, which was now nearly invisible for the snow. Soon he was at the stables.

Ansel should have felt relief at making it safely to a shelter, but a wave of anxiety hit him as he pushed open the heavy wooden door. There were a few dim torches lit, but no grooms came to greet him. Everyone knew that like his father, the prince was an avid horsemen. He surely would have left at least two groomsmen to watch over his favorite warhorses in such a storm.

"Hello?" Ansel called out. No one answered. His disquiet grew as he guided his horse into an empty stall. The other horses whinnied at him. They looked strangely thin for the king's animals. Peering closer, Ansel saw that they had feed in their troughs, but not much. The Fortress must be suffering from food shortages as well, he realized. In accordance, he took only enough to give his beast a few mouthfuls. He would pay the steward back when he found him. After brushing his animal and making sure he had clean hay, Ansel bundled back up to make the cold trek to the servants' entrance.

The Fortress's greeting was eerily similar to the one he received in the stables. When no one responded to his knocks, Ansel let himself in. As soon as the door was shut, he realized that not one candle was lit. Not only was it as dark as night, but it was just as quiet, too. No voices echoed down the stone halls. There were no whispers of children, or even footsteps to break the silence.

Something, a suspicious feeling kept him from calling out, so instead, he felt his way down the corridor to where he knew the servants' kitchen would be. There was one lone candle lit on the long wooden table and a weak fire in the large hearth. As long as Ansel had been visiting the Fortress to do business and speak with friends like the steward, there had always been people and food in this place. Women were always chasing giggling children away from the freshly baked bread, and hungry young men Launce's age were always hanging about looking for leftovers.

But now, aside from the small strange flames, there was no one. After a long, uneventful wait on the threshold, Ansel slowly walked into the large room. He found some old bread and aged cheese in one of the cabinets. The food was so dry it was nearly inedible, but Ansel was hungry enough to try and stomach it.

A flicker of light against the wall caught his eye. There was something about the way the shadow danced that unnerved him. It was too much like a human shadow. Shaking his head, he went back to eating. The exhaustion and cold must be getting to him, he thought. When the shadow moved again, however, more boldly this time, Ansel froze with food still in his mouth. Fear made his limbs feel strange, and he began to shiver harder than he had outside.

After a long moment of staring, he finally gained enough courage to swallow the rest of his bite. Standing up slowly, he faced the strange silhouette. It was really too large to be cast by the poor flames of the hearth or the candle. After he'd stared at it for a long moment, it moved again, jumping three feet down the wall toward the door. Another long minute later, it moved once more. Ansel got the feeling he was supposed to follow.

The game continued out of the kitchen and down the hall toward the servants' chambers. As he followed, Ansel got the feeling that this shadow wasn't the only one. The further he walked, the more invisible eyes he felt on him. Even stranger than that, however, was the sensation that the eyes were familiar. And though the situation should have sent him running back into the storm, he instinctively felt he could trust the strange apparitions. Either that, or the ancient food he'd just eaten was meddling with his ability to reason.

Unlike the shadows, however, the Fortress itself was as unfriendly as he'd ever seen it. The darkness was nearly suffocating. Walking in it felt like walking deeper and deeper into a tomb. The air was musty and damp, and it smelled as if neither a door nor window had been opened in decades. What had happened to the kingdom's beacon of shining light, the sacred place of protection? What kind of power could overcome it? This thought set him trembling more than anything else he'd encountered. Perhaps the gossip was not as farfetched as he'd first believed.

The shadow kept him moving quickly down the corridors, but he paused before the throne room. There was one light, the brightest of any he'd seen yet that shone through the high windows above the throne. All the other windows were covered, their tapestries drawn closed. It was moonlight, Ansel realized, that was coming through the highest of windows. The storm must have abated.

As his eyes began to adjust to the new light, he realized the grand room had been decorated and left that way. He could only guess it had been set for the great coronation ceremony, as that was the night everything had gone dark. He had turned to go back into the hallway when a voice spoke from behind him.

"And how is it that a commoner escaped the curse of the Fortress?" Ansel slowly turned to see that the throne, though hidden in shadow from the moon's rays, was not empty. A dark figure sat hunched in it. Its voice was soft and terrible.

"I beg your pardon, my lord?" Ansel timidly called back.

"All of my servants, my soldiers, and even my home itself were cursed into this blackness. No one has come nor gone for months. And yet, you come in as if you own the place.

"I beg your forgiveness, Sire," Ansel quickly knelt and bowed his head. So the prince *had* survived. "I sought shelter from the storm. If I'd stayed outside I would have died. I did not mean to intrude."

"What is your name?"

"Ansel Marchand of Soudain, Your Highness."

"And what are you doing out in such a storm?"

"I sit on Soudain's city council, and I was sent to visit other parts of the land to inquire about their matters of trade."

"So you thought it would be acceptable to trespass on sacred ground for this?" At this question, Ansel swallowed hard, praying his response would not be considered inappropriate.

"I beg your pardon, Sire, but was the Fortress not a place of asylum for the weary in the days of old?" The prince thought for a moment.

"It does seem that the Fortress has spared you, though I cannot understand *why*. But perhaps," The prince spoke slowly, "you can be of use to me." Ansel's heart skipped a beat. What on earth could the prince need with him?

"But first, I need to know why you were willing to enter a place that is cursed. What makes your life so worth living that you are willing to risk meeting with phantoms?" Ansel's words stuck in his throat. After narrowly escaping the royal edict meant for Isa, he could not tell the prince about his family. So he remained silent. "You would defy your prince?" For the first time, the terrible voice rose in tone, which made it only more awful. Still, Ansel would not speak.

"If you are unwilling to answer me, I will have no choice than to find out for myself. I supposed you have heard of my strength?" Of course he had. Though few knew how the monarchs' power worked, everyone knew their kings, and sometimes their queens, wielded a special gift. It had been the very reason Destin was the most feared kingdom in the realm. And it was most definitely not the kind of power Ansel wanted involved with Isa. Everard continued.

"It wouldn't be difficult for me to find whomever or whatever you're protecting. It also wouldn't be difficult for me to share the sickness of this place with them." This was more than Ansel could take. Defenseless against such a threat, he closed his eyes and spoke, his voice barely above a whisper.

"I have a family, Your Highness. I promised them I would come home safely."

"Tell me about this family."

"You wouldn't be interested in the family of a common merchant, Sire. We are much like other families of our kind." The prince thought for a moment before replying,

"No, I don't think you are. You're too careful, too protective of them. Oh come now, don't be so surprised. I've given my life to studying strategy and defense, and you, Tradesman, are putting up all your defenses. Now, I truly do want to hear about your family. As you can guess, I get few visitors at the moment. Entertain me." Ansel swallowed hard before answering. King Rodrigue had despised weakness, and after his son's attempt to weed out Ansel's daughter, it appeared the prince despised it as well. Ansel chose his words carefully.

"My wife is a shrewd woman, and runs my store as well as I do. She has also taught all of the children to be of use there. The youngest, Megane, is just a child, but she already shows a talent for weaving. Launce, my boy, is twenty, and he's training to take over the mercantile one day. My oldest daughter . . . ," Ansel's voice faltered for a moment. What if the prince knew her name? What if he remembered her? "My oldest daughter has a strong heart and a quick mind like no other." The prince held up his hand, and Ansel stopped.

"A strong heart, you say. What is this daughter's name?" Ansel faltered again before answering.

"Isabelle, Sire."

"And what about her heart makes it so strong?" The prince's voice was cynical, but Ansel detected a keen interest in it. His heart pounded as he struggled to answer Everard's question.

"She . . . suffered an injury as a child, but she never gave up. She was determined to be strong once again, and she is. Isabelle never gives up hope." Ansel prayed that would be the end of the prince's interest in his daughter, that the assurance of her strength and productivity would be enough, but he had no way to know. The prince's expressions were hidden in the dark. It seemed like a very long time that the two men sat there in silence, one kneeling and the other hunching in his throne. Finally, the prince spoke.

"So, Ansel Marchand, I have an assignment for you." His voice was quiet and terrible again.

"Yes, Sire?"

"When the road is clear enough to return, you will go back to your home. Isabelle will gather her things and say goodbye to her family and friends. Then you will bring her back here to me before dusk on the third day. Three days should be more than enough time for her to do so properly." It was as if Ansel's heart had stopped and his lungs had collapsed. He fought for his voice as he threw himself at his prince's feet.

"Your Highness, please! There must be some mistake! Take me! I will stay here in the stead of your servants! I will do anything you ask of me! But this I cannot do!"

"You can," the prince said testily, "and you will."

"No!" Ansel rose to his feet, his voice shaking as rage overcame his fear. "I will not give my child to you! You may sit here in the darkness of your great Fortress, but outside of it, you are nothing! If you were, the trade routes would no longer be filled with robbers and vagabonds, and Destin would once again thrive! You, Sire, cannot make me do such a thing!"

"Oh, but I can. Have you forgotten my threat? I may not leave the Fortress, but that doesn't mean my power is limited by gates or byways or walls. With just a wave of my hand, I can send this dark sickness upon your whole family as well. I'm sure your daughter who is strong of heart wouldn't want such a thing to befall her brother or sister or mother. No, sir, I don't think you're willing to risk your entire family's well-being for that of one."

Ansel's knees gave out, and he collapsed onto the cold stone floor, cursing himself for ever setting foot in the wretched citadel. It would have been better if he'd died in the storm.

"Take him away," the prince flicked his hand, and invisible beings grasped Ansel by the arms and dragged him out of the throne room. The unseen hands were gentle as they laid him in a bed that smelled of dust. He struggled to get up, but they firmly held him in place. Eventually, he could fight no longer and his fatigue won, but even in sleep he could not escape the torment of the guilt that consumed him.

In the middle of the night, he was awakened by an idea that had slipped errantly into his dreams. Cautiously he sat up. It appeared the shadows had left him alone once he'd stopped struggling. Silently, he hurried to put on his boots and winter coverings. They were not entirely dry yet, as the fire the shadows had built in his room was very weak, but he hardly noticed. There *was* a way to get Isabelle safe.

In three days' time, she and the rest of the family would be far away, and the prince would have to end these vile, constant attempts on her life. Ansel wondered if the prince knew about his attempted escape as he sneaked out to his horse. The animal stamped its feet, seeming as desperate to leave the place as he was. Less than an hour later, they were on their way. Snow had made the mountain road nearly impassible, but the merchant could not have cared less. Isa would be safe, his family would be together, and Heaven help the man that tried to stop him.

CHAPTER 5

In the months since the almost wedding, Megane had tried her best to stay out of Isa's way. Launce had stopped his teasing and replaced it with muttered threats about what he would do if he ever got his hands on Raoul. Deline had taken over Isa's hardest chores, and had suggested as many ways as she could think of to get Isa out of the house. Picnics were planned, the horses were taken for rides in the country, and her favorite dinner was made more often than ever before. Despite their well-laid plans, however, outings were quiet and awkward as the other three attempted to draw her into their jokes and stories.

To Isa, there was simply little to say, and everything that should be said could be spoken at home. Leaving the house was perilous, fraught with reminders that other people were still living their lives, happy, continuing to move through time. That Raoul was still living his life in the city without her. To Isa, time would stand still forever.

The most disastrous of their attempts to get her outside happened on the Marchands' own front porch, four months after Ansel had set out on his journey. There had been a snow the night before, ridiculously early for the season. Still, the ground looked pretty all covered in white, and Deline hoped the new scene might cheer her daughter. So Isa had been goaded into accompanying her mother to the tailor's shop, much to her disdain, and they were just returning when Margot, their neighbor, caught up with them. As the plump little woman ran toward them, the look on her face promised juicy gossip. Sure enough, before any greetings could be exchanged, Margot was speaking.

"Have you heard?" Her voice nearly squeaked with excitement. "Have you heard about young Master Raoul?" Though she managed to keep her eyes on the ground, Isa's heart beat unevenly. Out of the corner of her eye, she saw her mother give her an uneasy look.

"Isa, why don't you go inside and prepare some tea? I could use a warm drink, and I believe our guest could use one, also." But Margot shook her head, her words tumbling out faster than Isa could walk.

"No, I believe Miss Isa should hear this, and she'll know just how fortunate she is not to have married that horrible young man."

"Margot, I–" her mother tried to interject, but the older woman just kept talking.

"I was just down to the butcher's shop this morning when Harriet Bissette skipped into the town square to show off her ring. Can you believe it, Isa? He gave her exactly the same ring that he gave you!" His grandmother's ring. Isa's thumb instinctively moved to rub the spot that for six months had been occupied by the silver band. Not so long ago, he'd placed that ring on her own finger. Suddenly, it was hard to breathe.

". . . Less than a year, and he's already proposed to a second girl!"

"Really, Margot!" Deline protested, but their neighbor babbled on.

"Isa, you should count it a blessing that you two were not wed! You have a lovely face, my dear, but with your lame leg and hand and all, you wouldn't have been able to hold him. Better to be alone and keep your dignity than to know your man is off chasing other women because you can't satisfy him!" And with that, she spotted another neighbor who might not know the news, and was gone before Isa or Deline could say anything else.

Isa bolted for the door before any other well-intentioned friend or relative could find her and ran upstairs as quickly as her ankle would allow. Deline was faster, however, and she followed her daughter into the attic before she could get the door closed.

"I don't want to talk about it!" Isa threw her things down on the bed and went to stare out the window.

"Isa, you knew it was bound to happen."

"That doesn't mean I want to hear about it. This is why I don't leave the house!"

"You can't stay locked up in this attic forever. Listen, we've tried to be kind to you, to be sensitive to things that remind you of him. But you can't live the rest of your life hiding from the world!"

"What if I don't want to be part of the world?" Isa felt finally turned and faced her mother. "Thanks to our hero prince, the world thinks I'm good for nothing anyway! There's a *reason* all the women my age are expecting children, and their little sisters are getting married, and I'm not. Is it so much to ask that my nose not be rubbed in it? That I get to just stay where I'm wanted?"

"But you can't do that!" Deline was now just as loud as Isa, her voice quivering.

"And why not?"

"Because you were born for more than that!" Before Isa could reply, however, Launce burst into the room, out of breath.

"Mum, Isa, Father's home. Something's wrong." In a flash, Deline was downstairs. It took Isa longer to make her way down the wooden steps, but when she finally did, she could see that something was indeed wrong. Ansel's face was pale, and no matter how many blankets Megane and Launce piled on him, he shivered. What frightened Isa the most, however, was the wild feverish look in his eye. He looked like a dog cornered in an alley. It was ten minutes before his teeth stopped chattering enough to speak a single sentence, which was directed at Megane, asking her to take care of his horse.

"Let Launce do it," Deline told him as the girl bounded off. "She's been dying to see you, and the horse will take at least half an hour."

"I know," Ansel finally looked up from the tea they'd placed in his hands. "But I have something I must tell you all, and I'm afraid it will frighten her." At this, they all stopped what they were doing and stared. Isa felt a chill touch her heart. For though he spoke to them all, it was her he was looking at.

"We must pack what little we can with great haste. Take only what you need. I will send a message to Marko. We are leaving tonight after the sun sets." Dumbfounded, Isa looked at her mother and brother, but they seemed as much at a loss as she was.

"We're doing what?" Launce was the first one to find his voice.

"We're leaving with the Caregivers tonight. All of us."

"But . . . why?" Deline frowned.

"Father," Isa put her hands on her father's arm and knelt close to him. "What happened" Her touch seemed to calm him, but when his eyes met hers, they were wild with worry.

"Isa," his voice was hollow and old. "It's all my fault. I've done something terrible, and I cannot undo it. This is the only way I know how to save you. I . . . I was caught out on the mountain when the storm hit. I was afraid I would freeze, so I took the only familiar path I could find." Ansel swallowed loudly before looking beseechingly at the rest of his family. "I sought the shelter of the Fortress." The silence was deafening as a familiar feeling stirred in Isa's heart. She suddenly knew what kind of turn her father's journey had taken.

"The place is surely cursed," Ansel spoke again, shaking his head at his tea. "I used to laugh at such superstitions, but there was hardly a light in the entire stronghold."

"The servants?" Deline placed her hand over her heart.

"Shadows . . . Phantoms. I don't know. There are no bodies to serve the prince, but the spirits are certainly not lacking. And they do his bidding as well as any staff." He shivered with the memory. "And then there was the prince. I don't know how, but he somehow escaped the enchantment. At least, he still has a body. I couldn't see much for the darkness. He saw me, however, and he demanded to know about my family."

A sob suddenly wrenched itself from Ansel's body. "He said he would send a plague upon you all with his power if I did not obey! Isa, forgive me!" Her father dropped his tea cup on the floor and clutched at her hands desperately, his brown eyes desperately searching hers. "I tried so hard to shield you. I told him nothing of your injuries, only your strengths, and as little as I could. And yet, . . . he has demanded that you come to the Fortress to stay with him."

Horror washed over Isa. Even under a curse, would he never stop? Why couldn't he simply let her be? As the fear moved through her, however, it was quickly replaced with an even stronger emotion. How dare he? How dare this man threaten her family, using them as leverage to wage this strange war upon her?

"We can make him leave his hiding hole to come here and face us like a man! We could gather a militia!" Launce was fuming when Isa realized they were still talking.

"No, we do not know the true strength of his power," Ansel replied. "It would be best if we simply went with the Caregivers. They are our fastest way of escape. I don't think he'll be able to reach us on the third day if we leave tonight. We'll be nearly out of the kingdom by then." Isa quietly stood and slipped back up to her attic. Her family meant well, but their attempts would be fruitless. They didn't know the true power the prince wielded. She did.

The accident had taken place fourteen years before, when she was only nine, but the day was etched into her memory like writing on a tombstone. Lean and nimble, she'd weaved her way through the crowd to the street to see the handsome young prince as he rode by. She'd seen him from a distance a number of times when visiting the Fortress with her father, but this was the closest she had ever been to him. She'd been bumped from behind, however, and it sent her sprawling right into his horse's path.

How noble he'd looked when he jumped down to help her up. It took her a moment before she could shake the giddy fog from her mind, and by then he had left her side. Instinctively, she'd run and grabbed his sleeve, unaware at the time that it was inappropriate to touch a sovereign.

The pain had been excruciating, but what she'd never told anyone was that the pain hit before the horse's heavy hooves ever touched her. The moment he shook her off, a white hot pain had shot through her, as if he'd taken a branding iron and made her blood burn. The animal that had trampled her seconds later had left its mark for the rest of the world to see, but Isa could still recall the first pain more than that of her broken ankle and wrist.

If the prince had threatened her family, Isa had no doubt that he had the ability and the intentions to carry through with his plans, Caregivers or not. There was no other choice. Isa would have to go to the Fortress.

She nearly went back downstairs to tell her family when she quickly realized they would never listen. Her father would die before he let her go, and her headstrong brother would probably get himself killed as well. She would need to leave before they had a chance to try anything foolish. So she returned to the family, but stayed quiet. Her father was instructing them on how to prepare for their journey.

"We must bring as little as possible and go about our business as normal for the rest of the day. I don't want anyone aware that we're all leaving. Only the Caregivers themselves will know."

"And our mercantile?" Everyone turned to see little Megane standing in the doorway, her face white.

"I'm sorry, Megs," Ansel sighed and held his arms out to her. "I didn't see you standing there. No, we will have to leave our shop. But it will be alright. We will have one another, and we will set up a new life in the new land where Marko takes us. But we must not tell anyone, you understand? Anyone at all." Megane nodded seriously, her golden curls and round blue eyes shining brightly in the fire's light. "That's my girl," Ansel put his hand gently on her head before dismissing them all to do as they were told.

With a tight throat, Isa managed to grab both of her parents in a hug before gathering her things. They hugged her back, but Isa was sure they simply believed her to be afraid. They didn't know it was probably the last embrace they would ever share.

Wiping her suddenly watery eyes on her sleeve, Isa finally turned and headed back to her room. She had few belongings of any real value. A silver hairbrush from her parents and a change of clothes were all she could find to put in her bag. Megane had left her own bag open on her bed, so Isa slipped her favorite childhood doll inside of it. Her sister had always admired it, and though Megane was nearly too old for dolls, she might find it a comforting reminder of Isabelle after she was gone.

She needed an excuse to leave the house, particularly as her father had just returned with such urgent news. Immediately, her thoughts went to her horse. After losing her ability to run and dance, Ansel had taught his daughter to find respite in the freedom of riding. It had become a way of escape for Isa over the years, giving her a chance to feel the wind rush past her as she moved unhindered over the earth. Her parents would think nothing of her spending one last evening in the countryside with her horse.

"I'm going out for a ride," Isa finally announced to her family. It took all of her will to steady her voice as she spoke. "I . . . I need to think." They nodded understandingly, and her mother threw her favorite green cloak around Isa's shoulders.

"Use mine. It's warmer than yours. We'll be leaving just after nightfall, so be back soon." Trying to smile, Isa nodded and headed out to the stable. Using the special step her father had made for her, she was soon on her horse and headed toward the mountain.

Isa had never feared the mountain. As a child, she'd run up and down its familiar face with her brother and friends like mountain goats. More hill than cliff, its slopes were gentle, and its peak was rounded off at the top. It would take a few hours to get to the Fortress because of the melting snow drifts that still stood from the night's storm, but the path would be easy enough to find. An ancient tree marked its beginning, towering over all of its counterparts. From there, the path ran right alongside a stream carved every spring by snowmelt.

It felt strange to begin up the path again. She hadn't visited the Fortress since the incident with the prince. It was too strenuous for her ankle, and her father thought it best if she wasn't near the prince. The last time she'd set foot on this path was when she was young and free, able to run and dance without a care in the world. And now she was headed right into the domain of the man who had taken it all from her, strong leg, strong hand, even her wedding.

Isa couldn't help but shudder as she tried not think about what he could possibly want from her. Did he know who she was, or did he simply choose to pour out his wrath on the first passerby he could find? Though the stories of the Fortress monarchs had always painted them with at least decent senses of honor and chivalry, Isa had heard stories of how the rulers of other lands treated their wives and concubines. She wondered if that was what he wanted of her. Isa was never left alone with her fear, however, for her anger at what he had done, what he might want her to do, burned deep inside as well.

As the slope got a bit steeper, Isa had to focus more on guiding her horse along the snowy trail. As they walked, Isa began to sense that she wasn't alone. She looked around warily, hoping to spot a harmless animal in the brush or the trees, but she could see nothing. The forest was silent. Not even squirrels chattered. She tried to focus on the road ahead, pushing her horse just a bit faster. The closer she got to the Fortress, though, the more she felt the prying eyes.

When she spotted the Fortress entrance, Isa thought she'd made it. Just at that moment, however, something large flew out of the bushes and slammed into her, knocking her off her horse.

"Launce!" she gasped as she stared up into the face of her brother.

"What are you thinking?" He angrily ignored her question. "I thought you might get curious, but I didn't think you'd actually be stupid enough to take the bait!"

"If you get off me, I'll tell you!" Launce sat back enough to allow her to stand up. Isa scolded herself silently. She should have known her brother wouldn't let her leave without a goodbye. Actually, she knew he wouldn't let her leave at all. That was why she'd slipped out of the house when she thought he was out visiting his sweetheart one last time. Apparently, he'd been able to read her better than she thought. Isa took a breath.

"Father might think we can outrun the prince's powers, but he's wrong." Launce stared back at her with unforgiving eyes.

"So I'm supposed to let you simply run off to live with the madman prince?" For the first time, Isa wondered if she would actually be able to follow through with her plan. Launce was strong, and though she was tall, he was a whole head taller. It would be nothing for him to pick her up and take her home against her will.

"Would you sentence Megane to a slow death of sickness and pain?" she asked. His eyes widened a bit, so she continued. "Because he's strong enough. Launce, I felt it! When the prince touched me in the street all those years ago, I felt his power! It was more painful than I can describe. I don't know what he wants me for, but I do know that I want none of it near Megane. Or Mother or Father. Besides, if I don't do as he says, do you think he'll really spare me? My fate is sealed either way."

Isa sighed and leaned against her horse. "But the rest of you have a chance, particularly Megs. Let me do this for her. Please don't take it away from me." Isa drew in a shaky breath and added, "I don't think either one of us could live with ourselves if something happened to her."

The icy look had melted off of Launce's face, leaving the torn, helpless expression of the little boy Isa remembered from long ago. She breathed an inner sigh of relief as she saw her words sink in. Launce had always been protective of her, but they had grown up as a team. Megane was, on the other hand, the baby. Pranks they'd played on one another were simply not played on her. The unspoken rule was that she was to be protected above all else. And this was Isa's only hope for convincing her brother to let her go. She knew she'd won when she saw tears welling up his eyes.

Without another word, her little brother pulled her into a hug, and Isa clung to him, the fear and anguish of separation suddenly crashing down on her.

"You *must* keep Father from coming for me," she sniffled into Launce's shoulder. "You have to remind him that whether I stay or whether I go, the prince will have me in sickness or captivity. I'll be a happier captive if I know the family is safe." Launce finally pulled out of the embrace, still glaring at her. But he helped her back up on her horse and gave her a stiff nod before turning back down the path.

Feeling even more alone than before, Isa turned off the main road and the Fortress came into full view. The great stronghold was nothing new to Isa. She'd visited it many times with Ansel as a child, but never had it been so empty. The lofty battlements looked cold and foreboding without the soldiers at their posts. And the great front gate was closed. It seemed the prince wanted her to ask permission before entering his domain, to be reminded of just how small and insignificant she was. The old resentment flared up as Isa stared at the distant, lofty gate. Prince Everard might be forcing her to come, but that didn't mean she was going to play by his rules.

Isa turned her horse abruptly away from the front entrance. Skirting the outer wall, she headed around to the back of the Fortress, hoping the hole hadn't been patched up. The bushes had grown since she'd last visited, but to her relief, the gap hadn't been discovered. The servant children had shown her the opening in the outer wall once, how they used it to get in and out of the Fortress without their parents' knowledge. It was covered by a dense thicket of foliage, barely big enough for Isa's horse. But once she made it through, she was very glad she'd come this way.

Much less intimidating, the servants' entrance was smaller and had fewer grandiose architectures. If she'd gone further down the road, Isa would have made it to the servant's gate. What had been open for her father, however, must have been visited by some sort of spirit keeper, for the back gate was now closed. Isa rode through the open fields, noticing for the first time a strange set of great statues that filled half of the meadow behind the Fortress.

They seemed innumerable, large effigies lined neatly up in perfect rows and columns. Snow covered most of the figures, but there was something eerily human about them. They most definitely hadn't been there when she was little. Each one had unique features, carved of stone and yet giving the impression that they could get up and walk away whenever they pleased.

Isa finally arrived at the royal stables, where she took as long as she possibly could to feed and groom her horse. As she worked, she seriously considered sleeping in the stable. Her animal was warm and familiar. He was safe. But, Isa reminded herself, she had not abandoned her family to hide in a stable. She had come with a purpose, and no one would be safe until she fulfilled it.

"Good night, my dear friend," she softly rubbed the horse one last time. "I'll come see you as soon as I can." And with a deep breath and a prayer, Isa left the stable and headed for the servants' door of the Fortress.

The moment Isa crossed the threshold, her nerve nearly fled. The sun was almost set behind her, but the darkness before her was thick and terrifying. It was like a black fog had filled the once pristine, shining marble halls. The air smelled deeply of mildew and dust. After letting the door close behind her, she simply stood there, hoping her eyes would somehow adjust to the blackness. Somewhere deep down, despite her fear, Isa hoped this entrance would annoy the prince. She couldn't bear to give him the satisfaction of making her feel insignificant. Not any more than he already had, at least.

Isa finally found one single candle sitting on a table not far from the door. She nearly lost both the candle and her balance, however, when something cold brushed her arm. Her hand shook a bit as she held the flame up, trying to see what had touched her. There was nothing but the empty hall to see. Isa nearly screamed when two more breezes gave her gentle pushes from behind.

It was then that she remembered Ansel's warnings about the shadows. Drawing Deline's cloak about her as tightly as she could, Isa decided it would be best to do as they wished. Ansel had seemed to think they meant him no harm, but he really hadn't been there long enough to know for sure. Isa was pushed through a number of large empty halls and up several flights of stairs before she was allowed to rest. To her relief, a door was finally opened that led not into another hall or passageway, but rather a small room with a dim fire in a large hearth.

The fire didn't completely chase away the darkness, but it lit the room enough that Isa could see that it had once been a very grand room. The tapestries and carpets that were now filled with moth holes and covered in dust had obviously once been very beautiful, and were most likely made of rare fabrics. An oversized bed with tall posts at each corner filled much of the room, its head against the wall, next to the fire. A large wooden writing desk was placed near the windows that faced south.

"Thank you," Isa whispered to the shadows, a tear coming to her eye as she recognized the lights of Soudain in the distance at the foot of the mountain. There were the sentries, the ones that stood guard at the town entrance at night with their torches. Her father had been right. The shadows at least weren't malicious. If she was to be trapped in this place, at least she could sleep with her beloved city in sight.

That seemed to be the end of the shadow's kindnesses, however. Before she knew it, Isa was being pushed over to a large wardrobe in the corner of the room. She gasped as it opened on its own to reveal a large variety of dresses. Like the once lavish room, these gowns had been incredibly beautiful at one time. But they, too, smelled like wet dust. Isa stared stupidly at them for a moment before she realized why she was there.

"Am I supposed to put one of these on?" She felt silly asking the empty room. In response, however, the shadows nudged her one step closer to the wardrobe. "These are all far too extravagant for me," she shook her head. "I don't need anything like this." Again, she received a push. It seemed she had no choice. After glaring behind her, hoping the shadows would catch her annoyance, Isa picked the simplest of the gowns. If she was going to be introduced to the man who had tried three times now to steal her life, she would not be made a fool in princess's rags.

The gown she chose was simple but still luxurious. It was dark blue with a white bodice, with intricate silver stitching adorning the skirt just below the waist. Despite the craftsmanship, however, the dress smelled as awful as the rest of the Fortress. Still, Isa was forced to wear it. She could feel pulls and pushes at her sturdy boots, but she refused to let those leave her feet. She wasn't entirely sure that she'd be able to walk through the length of the palace without them.

"You can do anything else to me that you wish," she scowled at the fussing shadows, "but those aren't coming off until I'm ready for bed." Eventually, they left her boots alone and began to fuss with her hair, which admittedly, was rather messy from her journey up the mountain in the cold wind.

Finally, she was ready. Isa was getting used being pushed or pulled from all directions, so she went willingly when they prodded her out the door once more. This time, much to her relief, the halls were just a bit brighter. Someone or something had lit torches and placed them along the walls. With light now to walk by, she moved somewhat confidently. Until she walked right into the prince.

His shout of surprise was the first real sound Isa had heard since leaving her horse. It mingled in the air with her own startled cry as they both fell back a step. Immediately, Isa half knelt, half fell into a curtsy. As much as she meant to be brave, a deep fear quickly wriggled into her heart. She would soon find out what awful plans he had for her, and she suddenly didn't know if she could bear it.

"Your Highness!" her voice quivered strangely. "I apologize." It took him a moment to recover his own voice, but when he spoke, it was surprisingly rich, rude as his words were.

"Are you Isabelle?"

"Yes, Sire." As if any other sane woman would sneak into the cursed citadel. An awkward silence ensued as she continued to kneel and he stood over her. Finally, he demanded to know why she hadn't arrived during the day.

"I beg your pardon?" Isa had to keep herself from looking up in response to the strange question.

"I told your father that you needed to come during the day!" His voice was petulant. Isa had nothing to say to this. "He didn't tell you, did he?" the prince asked. Isa shook her head. "You came on your own, didn't you?" For fear of giving away her family's plans, Isa remained quiet. There was another long pause before the prince cleared his throat, his voice a little less sullen when he spoke again.

"Isabelle, you may stand when I talk to you from now on. I dislike speaking to the floor." As she stood, Isabelle dared to look at her prince for the first time in fourteen years. She nearly gasped aloud. He was the nothing like she'd expected. His hands were hidden in the folds of his clothes, but the part of his chin that showed was thin and pale, nearly chalky. Most of his face was hidden by the hooded cloak he wore, but even through the thick fabric, she could see his nearly emaciated frame. He was so bent he was nearly the same height that she was.

With a start, she also realized he stood and moved the way her grandfather had done before he died. But her grandfather had suffered from severe joint pain for years, and the prince should have been only twenty-seven, four years older than herself. It seemed her father had been wrong. The curse had touched the prince as well. This couldn't possibly be the hero prince the children sang songs about, the one who had slain dozens in battle. And yet, here he was.

"You weren't supposed to be here for two more days," he growled again. "How did you get in?"

"The servants' entrance, Sire," Isa tried to keep the small smile off her face. At least she had succeeded in doing something her own way. "I thought it only appropriate, as I'm to be your servant."

"It's true that–Look up at me," he interrupted himself, suddenly removing his hood. "I want to see you better." Isa couldn't have looked away if she'd wanted to. His face was gaunt. Dark circles seemed painted below his eyes, and his skin appeared fragile. It looked as if someone had stretched it too thinly over his sharp cheekbones. His golden hair was long and unkept, making his ashen cheeks look even more sunken.

But what really drew her gaze were his eyes. They were the only parts of his face that stood out more than his thin nose, but not because they were frightening as the rest of him was. The prince's eyes would have been gray if not for the thin rings of blue fire that encircled his pupils. They blazed in a strange, beautiful rhythm that made her want to look closer. Unfortunately, she realized, those beautiful, extraordinary eyes were suddenly glaring at her with a very real hatred.

He remembers me. So he hadn't brought her to the Fortress for revenge. The surprise and hate on his face was so intense that Isa would have wilted under it, had she not been battling similar feelings of her own. They stood glaring at one another for a long moment before his expression became more controlled. When he spoke again, his voice was slow and deliberate.

"Yes, you are my servant, but not the kind you think."

"Then, Your Highness, what am I here for?" He stared strangely at her for a minute longer before answering.

"You're here to help me break the curse." Isa nearly fell back a step. She had imagined many horrible endings to her time with the prince, but none of them had involved breaking a curse. She was both relieved and horrified.

"I can do that?"

"We'll see. Now, I assume you're tired from your journey. You will be served supper in your chambers tonight, but tomorrow, you will dine with me." And with that, the prince turned slowly and began to limp away. Still in shock, Isa stared as he paused one more time. "Oh, and one more thing. You are safe on the Fortress grounds by day, but you must never venture out after dark. I cannot protect you then."

CHAPTER 6

Shock, anger, and confusion clouded Ever's mind as he headed back up the tower steps, making it hard to think. It couldn't be her. It just couldn't. And yet, the crippled woman who had stood before him was injured in all the right places. Even more telling, though, were her eyes. The eyes that had haunted him for so many years, large and midnight blue, had been staring right up at him. From the moment he'd recognized her, it had taken all of his combat training to chase the angst from his face.

Of all the girls in the kingdom, why did she have to be the one? What kind of vengeful trick had that rat of a merchant played on him? He'd promised Ever a woman of strength and had given him a cripple instead. Ever contented himself with plotting how he would get even with the merchant until he remembered the desperation in the man's pleas when he'd asked to stay in his daughter's stead. Besides, Ansel had boasted of Isa's strength of heart; he'd said nothing of her body.

Ever considered this as he continued the slow climb up the stone steps. Could Isa's heart have the strength the Fortress demanded? If so, it certainly wasn't like his strength. She could barely get off the floor from her kneeling position, let alone fight a battle. And yet, there had been a spark in her dark eyes that had hinted at something fierce beneath the surface. There was nothing to lose, the voice of reason suggested to him, by allowing her to try.

It wasn't like he had any better ideas. In the months after the curse, Ever had very nearly gone mad. He'd shuffled around the Fortress in his new prison of a body, raving at the stone walls like a lunatic. The great Fortress, which had been his constant companion and guardian since childhood, had abandoned him. He no longer felt the familiar presence pushing or pulling him in different directions. There was no gentle guiding company, no personal familiarity with all that surrounded him. The sorrow he felt at losing his courtiers and servants was nothing compared to this. Losing his parents was nothing. For a while, all he'd wanted to do was die. If the Fortress was so intent on forsaking him, he had cried out, then why couldn't it simply let him die? Without the Fortress, Ever didn't know where he belonged or what his purpose was. Without the Fortress, Ever was nothing.

The servants, damned to existence as shadows, had kept him alive, somehow, but just barely. After days and nights of walking and screaming into the eternal night, he would awake to find himself in new clothes with food somehow in his belly. In time, he'd eventually realized that if he focused, he could sense their emotions. His real saving grace, however, had been the evening when he first heard Garin speak.

The day had been much like the others, one filled with Ever's rants at the Fortress, when the shadow that acted most like Gigi had forced a bowl of thin soup into his hands. Ever protested, but the shadow would not let him rest until he'd begun to eat.

"How does it taste, Sire?" Ever had very nearly choked on his food when Garin's composed voice first broke the silence. When he finally regained his composure, he demanded to know where the others were, hoping perhaps the curse was lifting on its own. But it wasn't to be. As always, the unusual steward had either found a way around the rule of silence, or was exempt from it. As disappointed as he was about the others, Ever was grateful for even this small improvement.

Still, life had seemed bleak and hopeless for a long time after that. The curse was a riddle, and he didn't know how to interpret it. *What has been broken must be remade.* That he was broken was obvious. Ever had never felt as vulnerable in his life as the moment he'd awakened inside a body that was no longer his. Every joint ached. He could no longer stand tall. His hands were those of an aged man, bent and clawlike in their pain. It was only with great difficulty that he could grasp objects, and the aching and swelling in his knees made it equally difficult to walk upright. The limbs that had subdued enemies and won battles had become frail and defenseless. He had become like the very people he despised, weak.

The one who was strong must be willing to die. He had been strong. But had he also not been willing to die? Ever had fought in countless battles alongside his father and his men. He'd faced adversaries of great evil. Surely this part of the curse would be the easiest to break. If only he could be remade, then he could prove his willingness to die. Which left the most confusing requirement of all.

A new strength must be found. This requirement had brought him countless nights of despair. Ever had always been filled with the strength of the Fortress. The light had burned brightly in his eyes since the day he was born, and it had filled the servants with hope. All of Ever's forefathers had possessed the strength, but according to Garin, none had ever possessed it the way he did. The strength was a part of him, just as the Fortress had always been. He didn't know how to live without it.

The first time Ever had begun to understand what a power he possessed was when he was young, only six. He'd told the master of swords that he wanted to learn how to fight. Greatly amused, the master of swords had given him a small wooden training sword and taught him a few blocks and thrusts. Ever had then challenged the man to a duel. A few of the courtiers and servants had come to watch, smiling with affection at their young, ambitious prince. The master had given him just a few gentle obvious thrusts and lunges when a blue fire suddenly burst from Ever's arm and down his sword. In the blink of an eye, the master of swords was on the ground, the breath knocked out of him as Ever stood over him with his little wooden sword.

After that, Rodrigue had to be the one to train Ever, as no one else had the strength to withstand him. As Ever had gotten older he'd learned better how to restrain the natural fire that came from within him. The power touched more than his body, however. He was also very sensitive to other people. He could tell when someone was lying immediately, and his parents found early on that they could not leave or enter the Fortress without his knowledge.

The strength that filled him had always inspired confusion, even fear in many. His father had approved of this and encouraged him to use it to his full advantage. He'd ended many battles before they were begun simply by intimidating enemies in a face-to-face meeting. What kind of strength could exist that compared to what he'd had? What new strength was there to appease this curse?

It almost didn't matter. Even Ever's strength had all but disappeared when the curse had taken effect. The blazing blue in his eyes had dulled until it was all but extinguished, and he was weakened, not just compared to what he had been, but by any man's standards. Ever couldn't even imagine where he was supposed to search for a new kind of strength. Besides, he didn't want a new strength. He wanted his old strength back. Still, he'd searched every piece of writing in the Fortress's Tower of Annals. Nothing had suggested itself as a possible new strength. Until the day Ansel had arrived.

It was the way Ansel had worded the description of his daughter that had suggested the idea to Ever. *She has a strong heart and a quick mind like no other*, Ansel had said. What if she could bring a new kind of strength, Ever had suddenly wondered. Perhaps the strength of her heart would be enough to satisfy the Fortress's demands. Then her strength could mend his body, the thing that had been broken. If he was whole again, he could prove that he was willing to die by facing Nevina, whose men were now camped at the foot of his mountain.

The memory of that night with the merchant filled Ever with shame, as it always did. Ansel's pleas for mercy had nearly moved him. Aside from his one night of too much drink, Ever had never considered threatening to kill a whole family simply to get his way, particularly with a sickness. It was the coward's way. But, he told himself, this was the only hope he'd found in the months of his searching. If it worked, it would be for the good of the whole kingdom.

Of course, there was the question of whether the young woman would cooperate or not. It was obvious that she hated him. He couldn't exactly blame her for that. His hasty, childish outburst had must have greatly altered her life. The rebellious defiance had been there in her eyes the entire time they had spoken. As much as he disliked her, Ever had to admit after the encounter was over that she was indeed not weak of heart. And that observation watered the seed of hope her father's words had planted within him. *She has a strong heart*.

Perhaps, with time and attention, Isabelle could be moved past her hate for him. He would need to treat her kindly, make her feel wanted. And he would definitely need to change his direct, blunt way of addressing her. That had seemed to make her angrier than anything else in the short time they'd spoken. But with lots of work and very carefully chosen words, perhaps there was a shred of hope that her strength was indeed what the curse demanded. A new strength.

As Ever laid down on his pallet and looked out the window at the north foot of the mountain, he felt the dangerous beginnings of hope spark inside him. Nothing could be sure, however, until he saw whether or not the Fortress had truly chosen her for her strength. And that test would have to wait until tomorrow night.

CHAPTER 7

Isa tossed yet again in a vain attempt to sleep, but the musty smell of the bed and the revelation of the prince's purpose for her kept her awake. What had possessed him to think *she* could help him unlock the secrets of the realm's oldest source of power?

Isa had heard the stories growing up, tales of the monarchs' strength, great feats of cunning and bravery that were only possible because of the Light of the Fortress, strength that was conceived from the Fortress itself. There were legends parents told their children at bedtime, but no one knew much beyond those legends. The true nature of the Fortress was unfamiliar to the people, something that wasn't given too much unnecessary attention. Tradition dictated that only the monarchs' truly understood their own power, and if the commoners were smart, they'd leave it that way. But Isa's childhood brush with the prince's power had long ago stirred something inside of her, and despite all her desire to return home and be rid of this devilish place, she found a small piece of her heart wishing to unravel this knot of mystery. She also found herself completely terrified. How was she supposed to address the power that had ruined her limbs? Even more importantly, how was she to even begin breaking the curse? And what would he do to her if she failed?

Isa rose early while the sky was still gray and listless. It was a morning typical of mid-autumn. Still, she noticed that perhaps for the light of the day, the smell of dust wasn't quite as strong as it had been when she laid down. *The morning is meant for deep breaths and new beginnings, Isa*, Deline would always say. And it seemed she was right.

As she managed to swallow the dry biscuit and old apple left on her bedside table by invisible hands, Isa realized her own clothes had been returned to her during the night. After getting dressed, Isa decided the first thing to do would be to find the Fortress annals. In the millennium since the Fortress had come into being, someone must have written something down about the great power it wielded.

"Please take me to the Fortress annals," Isa addressed the shadows. Instead of the familiar pushes and pulls she had grown somewhat accustomed to, however, she felt all the shadows disappear. Surprised and annoyed, Isa shook her head and begrudgingly wandered out of her room. She wasn't quite brave enough to look for the room on her own just yet.

Heading to the front of the stronghold, Isa saw the grand entrance for the first time. Covered in dust and cobwebs, giant columns soared above her supporting monstrous arches that were loftier than any church steeple in the city. The ceiling was so high and so dark that Isa couldn't make out any of its details at the very top. In fact, the interior was nearly as dark as it had been the night before, as all the tapestries were closed. She was again glad she'd arrived by the back entrance, for coming in through this entrance would surely have intimidated her. As she cautiously approached the towering doors, they opened for her without a sound.

Most of the snow from the storm two days earlier had melted, making Isa's walk to the stable much easier.

Isa spent as long as she could out in the stable, feeding and brushing her animal. It was comforting to breathe in his familiar scent. She talked to him as she worked, telling him what a good horse he was, and how he wouldn't believe the things she'd seen the night before. She took him for a quick outing, but was too nervous to take him very far. Eventually, there was no more she could do for him, so she put him back in the stables and wandered back to explore the front lawn.

The Fortress lawn had at one point been the most spectacular arrangement of gardens and statues one could ever hope to see. But now, beneath the melting snow, the flowers lay brown and brittle, as did the trees. Everything was overgrown or wasting away. Isa wandered through the ivy covered statues of wolves and the dying shrubs without knowing where she was headed. No birds sang and no chipmunks twittered. There weren't even the sounds of bugs as she moved through the gardens. Isa wondered if the gardens had always been this quiet or if the curse had made them that way. She'd nearly turned to head back to the stables when one garden in particular caught her eye. It was a rose garden.

The bushes had been allowed to grow tall, and had been planted in such a way as to provide walls of privacy for those who walked the paths laid in stone between them. It was impossible to see inside until one ventured down a path. Isa circled the large garden and found that there were four paths that wound toward the center, one for each direction. Despite the vines being brown and dry without a flower to be seen, Isa found herself drawn to their beauty. She cautiously started down the northern path.

In the center and along the walkways, the bushes stood at least three feet higher than Isa's head. A small courtyard lay in the center of the garden, large enough it could have fit her new bed inside of it. A stone bench made of multicolored stones sat along the edge of the tall, pruned bushes where it would have been hidden from the sun had the sun been shining.

In the center was the most beautiful stone mosaic Isa had ever seen. A rose larger than Isa was tall had been carefully laid out with multicolored stones. Agate gave the rose its shades of red, while Jade pieces filled the leaves and stem. It was all encircled by blue Angelite and white opal. Every single stone had been polished down to make the surface of the path perfectly flat. A small flame of rebellion was suddenly ignited inside of Isa, and the longer she looked at it, the more the flame grew. If she couldn't go home, and she couldn't visit the annals, then she would dance.

Slowly, she walked to the center of the mosaic. It looked like it should be hidden from the main path, but she peered around anyway. Hopefully the shadows weren't watching. Gingerly, she extended her right arm, then as well as she could, she pointed her left foot. Before she finished the first twirl, Isa's ankle gave out, and she collapsed into a heap on the cold stone. Angry tears welled up in her eyes as she imagined how her former peers would have laughed at her if they could see her now. Her neighbors would have shaken their heads sympathetically, and even her parents would have urged her to stop before she hurt herself. The shame was still just as strong as it had been the day the healer told Isa she would never dance again.

But they aren't here, a voice inside her whispered. It didn't matter if the girls she'd once danced with would laugh, and it didn't matter how many times she fell. Isa was all alone now, and there was no one to stop her. Wiping the tears from her eyes, she stood up resolutely and stretched her arms out again. A small seed of hope began to sprout in her heart as she slowly recalled the steps and turns in time.

With each movement, her body once again remembered the fluid energy that had once flowed through it. Her form was stiff, and nothing about her movements looked effortless or graceful. Her left wrist couldn't lay straight, and her ankle was too weak for the leaps. And yet, in spite of herself, Isa began to smile. Sweat ran down her back and soaked her dress, and her hair fell out of place. But for just a moment, nothing in the world could have made her happier.

Isa danced until her ankle nearly gave out. Finally, she fell onto the stone bench to rest. Only then did she realize that one of the shadows must have brought her lunch. It was simple lunch and so dry she could hardly swallow it, as it had been that morning, but Isa's hunger drove her to eat it all.

"Thank you," Isa called out to whatever phantom had thought to bring her food all the way out in the rose garden. She expected no reply but was pleasantly surprised when a quick breeze gently brushed her cheek. Knowing her ankle would last no longer, Isa stood up and limped back to her room, where she dozed until the shadows awakened her in time for supper.

Isa had been dreading supper with the prince. Not only had he ruined her life on more than one occasion, but he also seemed quite haughty. Isa's manners were by no means lacking, but court etiquette was something she had never learned, and she did not want to give him another reason to look down upon her.

As the shadows began to brush her hair, a large bath on the other side of the hearth was drawn. Isa hadn't noticed it there before. A warm bath would be nice, she thought, until she walked over to it and realized the water was just as dirty as the rest of the Fortress was. She balked.

"You can't mean for me to wash in that. I'll be filthier when I get out than when I get in." In response, some brave shadow snatched up a rag, dipped it in the water, and began to vigorously scrub one of her arms. Isa let out a little cry as the cold water touched her skin. Taking their cues, other shadows began to do the same. Apparently, her unwillingness to get in was not a problem for them. Muttering at the shadows, Isa cringed throughout the entire bath, snatching away the drying cloth when it was finally presented to her. Then, as she had been the night before, Isa was dragged over to the wardrobe of musty dresses to choose one.

"Where is the one I wore last night?" She gave a doubtful look at the rest of the fancy dresses that hanged before her. Her answer was a light shove that brought her one step closer to the wardrobe. "Just so you know," she grumbled, rifling through the piles of lace and frills, "I'm not keen on all this finery. Your prince brought me here as a servant, and a servant's wear is much more what I would prefer to appear in."

The shadows paid no heed to her speech, however. They snatched the gown that Isa had chosen out of her hands, and then pushed her over to the writing desk, which had been quickly transformed into a vanity. Deft, invisible hands pulled her hair up into intricate curls and tucked them neatly into one another, while other sets of hands did their best to brush the dirt off the burgundy and cream dress. Another draped a necklace of dull red Agate around her neck.

When the shadows were finally satisfied with her hair and jewelry and gown, Isa looked around for her boots. Her heart fell into her stomach when she realized the only shoes she could find were red velvet slippers.

"Where are my boots?" she cried out. The invisible hands, still adjusting her hair here and there, paused, but then continued as if she hadn't spoken. Her voice got a bit louder as she asked again. "Where are my boots? You cannot mean for me to wear these!" When she again received no response, Isa pulled up her skirts to reveal her crooked ankle. "I can hardly walk without those boots! I don't know how you expect me to get to supper if I cannot walk! Now please, give me my boots back!" But the boots never appeared, and nothing Isa said or threatened to do made them reappear. Finally, she was bullied out of the room without them. Defeated, she took three times as long to reach the dining hall as she would have if her own boots had been worn.

Prince Everard was already seated by the time Isa arrived. She could tell by the gentle windy shoves to her back that she was late, but she didn't care. Perhaps that would teach them to think twice next time they wanted to give her such foolish shoes.

"Isabelle," Everard stood slowly when she entered the room.

"Your Highness," Isa gave him the best curtsy she could manage before collapsing into the chair after her long trek. When they were both seated, unseen servants placed food on the table before them. The light was a little better in this room because of the multiple fireplaces that were lit and the candles that were scattered about the table. She supposed it was probably polite for the guest to praise something about the home or the food or the décor to the host, but Isa could think of nothing to say. Still angry about the boots, and reminded of how much the prince irritated her, Isa stared sullenly at her plate, sneaking angry looks at her host every so often.

He still wore the long, thick cloak. Isa presumed it was to cover a nearly skeletal body that would have matched his face and neck. His dark gold hair had been cut much shorter than it had been the night before, and it now shined weakly in the firelight. The deep hollows under his eyes made it look as if he had constant bruises. It was hard to imagine that this man had ever fought against any foe and lived to tell the tale.

Everard finally spoke. His voice was distant, but surprisingly polite, very different in tone than it had been the night before.

"Your quarters are comfortable, I presume?"

"Yes, Your Highness."

"And the servants have provided you with what you've needed?"

"I suppose you could say that." Isa glared at the ground, thinking of how much her ankle already ached after walking from the bedroom. Another silence ensued as they tried to eat the bland stew that had been set before them, the clinking of their spoons making the lack of conversation even louder. Eventually, Everard took a deep breath before finally asking a question Isa could not give a simple answer to.

"So what do you think of the Fortress so far?" Isa's face began to burn as all the emotions that had been boiling inside her rose to the surface.

"It would be easier to fulfill my purpose here if I were allowed to visit your annals, but your servants this morning refused to assist me when I asked," she snapped. For a moment, the prince stared at her, surprise making his gray eyes look even larger in his gaunt face than usual.

"You think you are to break the spell by reading about it?" His fluid voice had a hint of amusement to it that annoyed Isa even more.

"Well I certainly wasn't raised here, and I know no more about the Fortress than any commoner. I don't see any other way to learn about it, and I can't be expected to break a curse I know nothing about!" Everard gave a low chuckle before putting his spoon down and leaning toward her over the table.

"Miss Isabelle, I am proficient in four languages, including the two dead tongues that existed before the birth of this land. I was trained to read the markings of the ancient symbols that were carved into the tombs of my forefathers. I have had access to the sacred writings all of my life, and I've been living alone in this great crypt for six months. What do you think I've been up to during that time?" To that, Isa had no response.

"Believe me," he continued more seriously, "if the curse could be broken by *reading*, I would have found it by now." Holding her resentful gaze, he added, "I have ordered my servants to give you full access to the Fortress so that you know my good will. Except the Tower of

Annals. The Tower of Annals is mine, and even the servants have restricted access to that place. Only a few are allowed to accompany me there." Isa wondered how he knew which shadows really did accompany him there, but she didn't ask. Instead, she found herself still protesting her lack of books.

"I still know nothing of this place or its true history. I can't even begin to consider how I am to break the curse if I am completely ignorant!" At this, Everard's annoyance seemed to surface on his face for the first time, which up until now, had been a mask of cool reserve.

"Ask the servants for any specific books you require, but by no means are you to enter the Tower of Annals. Do you understand?" Isa nodded. For a moment, the blue fire in his eyes flashed, and in spite of herself, Isa felt a bit frightened. Briefly, she could see the warrior prince. Then the flashing dimmed and he slowly stood. As he walked over to her, he again reminded her of her aged grandfather. The prince extended Isa a black gloved hand.

"Miss Isabelle, would you do me the honor of dancing with me?" Isa felt her mouth drop open in horror and panic filled her. All of the confidence she'd fought so hard to convey slipped away in that instant, and before she knew it, she was begging, pleading not to dance. Tears ran down her face as she looked up at him.

"Your Highness, I have come here in accordance with your will! I have worn the dresses, eaten your food, and agreed to live in your home! Please don't humiliate me in this way. I beg of you!" As she wept, surprise showed in his eyes again, but he did not relent.

"This is something you must do if you wish to help me break the curse," he said quietly, but firmly as she sobbed. Still, she could not rise. Gently but resolutely, he reached down and took her hand, leading her out the tall dining hall doors to an outdoor balcony.

The balcony was huge, larger by far than the entire dining hall. Even more strange was the floor. Instead of the typical stone, it was covered by a beautiful, clear crystal. It lay as smooth as a pool of water, and unlike anything else in the Fortress or its grounds, was completely spotless. A hundred couples could have danced upon it. As they approached the center, invisible musicians began to play, their beautiful, haunting melody echoing over the mountain. As magnificent as the music was, however, Isa could not enjoy it.

They were an awkward couple, able to do little more than sway back and forth. It seemed the prince's knees were as stiff as Isa had suspected from the beginning. Her own ankle throbbed with pain as the little slipper left it completely unsupported. Isa was horrified to realize she had to lean slightly on her partner more and more as they continued to dance. They shuffled slowly in circles as the music played.

Worse than any of this, however, was the acute knowledge that Everard was only the second man who had ever been willing to dance with her. The warmth of his gloved hand on her waist and the closeness of his body to hers was nearly unbearable. It was too much like the last time Raoul had danced with her. They had been at a town festival, and his eyes had gleamed with joy as he'd twirled her in circles over and over, despite the disapproving looks of his parents. That had been the night he'd proposed.

Tears began once again to run down Isa's face, and she knew the prince was watching her curiously. Yet, he said nothing. By the time the dance was finished, Isa could continue no longer.

"I beg of you, Sire, if you have any pity in your heart at all, please just let me go. I cannot go on tonight." Isa hated appearing this weak in front of the prince. Her goal from the start had been to appear strong, to let him know that she was not a coward, nor was she coming willingly. But the pain of her ankle and the pain in her heart tonight were too much to bear. Nodding, he stepped back and bowed slightly. Isa didn't even attempt to curtsy as she did her best to begin limping back to her room.

CHAPTER 8

Ever left the balcony tired and sore, but pleased nonetheless. It had been worth the physical aches to know that his plan could indeed work. While they'd dance, he'd seen what the girl's untrained eyes could not, especially as she'd spent the whole time crying. Beneath her shuffling feet, the crystal had given off the barest hint of a blue glow. It certainly wasn't the bright shine that his ancestors had used to find their wives in the stories, so clearly she was not yet ready to be queen. But she could be. She truly had some sort of strength, enough to awaken the power of the Fortress that had seemed to all but disappear since the curse.

Back in the Tower of Annals, Ever stiffly sank into the warm bath his servants had prepared for him. He'd long ago ceased caring about the dirty water. The relief it brought his body was too great to sacrifice for some grime. Two of the shadows removed his gloves and began to gently rub a potent salve into them. He closed his eyes and leaned his head back, not wishing to ruin his good spirits by the sight of his claw-like hands, or any part of his body for that matter.

He was not used to the strain it took to dance, and the pain was enough to make his eyes prick. It reminded him all the more of why he must succeed in preparing this strange girl to carry the Fortress's power. At the rate his strength was leaving him, he would not survive the next spring.

After getting redressed, Ever slowly moved to his pallet, which had been laid out on a low sofa. Although his mood had improved with the revelation of Isabelle's potential, the fires at the north foot of the mountain sobered him once again. News of the darkened Fortress had spread fast, apparently, and Nevina had made her camp just a month after the curse had fallen.

The rogue Tumenian forces were still hurting from their last defeat. From the number of fires that burned, Nevina was still out gathering men, and would be for some time. If nothing else, Ever comforted himself, their last battle had produced a bit of fear in their northern enemies, one that would make them think long and hard before attacking hastily again. It would buy them some time. He just hoped it would be enough.

Ever laid down where he could watch the fires, but could not keep his thoughts on the princess's militia for long, despite his efforts. Instead, his mind kept wandering back to the strange girl across the castle. He'd been right when he first guessed she despised him. The flash of her eyes had not been lost on him when she spoke, and it seemed he was incapable of pleasing her. He found that this disappointed him for some reason. Of course, her willingness to carry the power of the Fortress would speed her strength, and for that, he desperately hoped. Still, he had hated her for so many years. Why was he interested at all in what she thought of him?

The strange desire for her respect had tugged at his heart earlier that day when he'd seen her dancing in the rose garden. She was by no means a lovely dancer, but there was something about her that had made him watch a few moments longer. He'd happened to look out of the tower windows to see her fall to the ground, and had nearly sent a servant to check on her, when she got up and tried again.

After spending so many years hating her for haunting his dreams, it felt wrong to see her as anything but a means to his end. And yet, he had to admit that after one day of having her as a guest in his home, he could see what her father meant when he'd said she had a strong heart. A woman who would willingly turn herself in to live as a servant in a cursed castle with the man that had made her lame as a child, that woman was worthy of respect. Getting up and continuing to dance after falling so hard was worthy of respect. A small voice in his head wondered if perhaps he had taken even more from the young woman than her ability to walk, but this wasn't something he was yet ready to consider.

He also found himself wondering at her reaction to dancing on the balcony. She'd spent her entire morning dancing. Why would she be so upset at dancing with him? It couldn't be that she was embarrassed. His bent back and weak knees made it obvious he would dance poorly. But then, he hadn't missed the way she'd shuddered when he touched her hand, or how her eyes had widened when he'd stepped into the bright moonlight. This also bothered him more than he wanted to admit, that of all the important pieces of the puzzle, his vanity was troubling him. But, he shook his head, there was nothing more he could do than go on with the charade.

"Garin," he called quietly.

"Yes, Sire?" Garin's shadow flitted to stand before him. Keeping his eyes on the fires below, Ever asked,

"What do you think of her?" The steward paused a moment before answering.

"In truth, Sire, your question isn't an easy one to answer. I've known young Isabelle since she was a child, before the accident even." Ever couldn't conceal his shock as he whipped his head around to look for the familiar face that wasn't there.

"You never told me that!"

"My apologies, Your Highness, but you were young, and struggled greatly with the incident yourself. I didn't want to make you even more anxious about it."

"She was the one you went to warn on the night of the coronation, wasn't she?" Ever asked softly. He hadn't missed the sudden disappearance of his steward, as well as many of his other officials. He'd been drunk, but the details of all that he'd said and done that night were burned into his memory.

"Yes," Garin's voice was quiet, too. "I knew her father." A few moments later, Ever asked him another question.

"How can I win her heart? I need her to accept the Fortress and myself in order to best carry the strength. It will be very difficult to do that if she hates me as she does now. If she can develop the strength, however, we can be married, and our strength can unite to end all of this."

"Be careful, Everard," Garin's voice had a sudden edge to it. "She is not like the court women you are familiar with. Her past and her present have put her in a very delicate place." Ever didn't bother asking how Garin knew such things. Just as Garin's origins were unknown, his methods of getting information were mysteries best untouched as well. The steward continued speaking.

"And if the Fortress has brought her here, then it has an interest in her, and nothing good will come of meddling vainly with her heart. She is one who cannot be easily purchased." A moment later, Ever heard Garin sigh, and when he spoke again his voice was more resigned.

"Her father was here on a business matter not long before the Fortress went dark. He told me that a young man had recently begun to draw her from her sorrows, but from the look in her eyes tonight, that future she envisioned with him is no more. Reaching her . . . It will take time and sincerity. Pushing her before she's ready will only hurt you both."

"I don't have the time for sincerity," Ever retorted.

"And what will you do, Sire, if she refuses you? Will you force her into wedlock against her will?"

"Garin, I'm asking you for your help so that's never a problem!" Ever huffed. The conversation had taken a turn he didn't like, and Garin's tone of a loving mentor was grating on his ears. "She is strong, Garin. She *must* be the one to bring the new strength, to heal me, to make me ready to face death again and break the curse! Besides," he added sulkily, "even if she's not madly in love with me, I'll be giving her more than any woman from her station could ever dream of. She'll be queen, surrounded by every luxury she could ever imagine, and the Fortress's strength, too."

"Neither gold nor power cannot mend a broken heart," Garin said gently.

"Well, then," Ever frowned at the shadow, "it's your job to find me something that can."

CHAPTER 9

When Isa awakened the next morning, the sun had already risen high in the winter sky. Wiping sleep from her eyes, Isa struggled to break free of the dreams that had trapped her all night. Images of Raoul and the prince had blended together into a terrifying nightmare, a never ending dance in which she was both unwanted and yet forced to be a part of.

It was a few minutes before Isa was completely convinced the visions were dreams. As she began to recall the details from the night before though, she wasn't sure the truth was any better than the dreams had been. The silken slippers, the lonely dance, and the hopelessness came back to her piece by piece. And as each miserable moment returned, a new determination began to set in.

Never again would she be a part of that story. She was through letting the shadow servants bully her, no matter how many orders Prince Everard gave them. She wasn't going to wear the slippers; it would be her boots or no dancing at all. And if indeed the prince wanted to dance again, she would choose to hold her head high, not lower it in shame with tears running down her face. Maybe her mother had been right. There was a time to mourn what she had lost, but she could see now that self-pity had made her weak and vulnerable. She would never be powerless like that again.

In addition to her new sense of resolve, Isa had begun to sense a strange new presence. Despite her terrible dreams, she'd felt just a little less alone that night as she slept. Oddly, she innately knew that the presence which comforted her didn't belong to any of the servants who were always hovering nearby. It was a different kind of comfort, more potent than any human company she'd ever encountered. And as much as she was confused by it, the new presence had somehow transformed the Fortress in her eyes overnight. The smells of dust and mildew were noticeably less powerful, and the bed she slept in had felt just as familiar as the one in her parents' attic.

The presence didn't fade as she got dressed. Her boots and clothes had been once again returned to her during the night. Isa took the new shine of her boots as a sort of apology from the servants.

"I accept your apology," Isa announced to the shadows as she pulled the boots on. "But don't think that means you can take them again tonight. If the prince wants to dance, I'll be wearing the boots or there will be no dance at all, understand?" The shadows brushed by her in annoyed, sharp breezes, and Isa felt a sense of laughter from the walls around her. What was this strange presence that heard both her words and her heart?

"Oh," she called out once more to the servants, knowing they would listen even if they didn't want to. "And tell your prince I need books on the early history of this place. That should be a mild enough request to suit him."

The sense of the presence still didn't depart as Isa left her room. Instead, it felt close, warmly wrapping around her the way her mother's cloak did. Moving through the towering halls and out to the stable, it felt like the presence had been there her whole life. How had she missed it before this? It was as if her eyes were just being opened.

After tending to her horse, Isa returned to the rose garden. As confirmation of her suspicions that something was different, there was a single rose bud on the hedges when she arrived. It was near the place she had fallen the day before. The flower was small, to be sure, and hardly open, but the bright sliver of pink was impossible to ignore against the background of brown.

"What is this place," Isa murmured to her new companion, "that rose buds should bloom just before the dawn of winter?" In response, a breeze smelling of lavender caught her dress and twirled it gently against her legs. Isa smiled, remembering what she'd come to the garden for. Her ankle bore none of the pain from last night, strangely enough, and was now tucked safely in her boots. It was time for her to dance.

Once again, Isa's dancing was not the fluid, confident movement it had been when she was a child. In fact, her limbs were sore from the day before, and possibly even less coordinated. And yet, her arms, her legs, and even her ankle felt just a little more poised, a little more prepared for the steps she put them through.

A few hours later, as she headed in for lunch, Isa realized with a start that for the first time in years she felt like she had a purpose here. And as much as she hated being held against her will, and even if the prince *was* a despicable human being, she desperately wanted a purpose, one that went beyond tending her parents' store for the rest of her life. If she was somehow able to miraculously restore the Fortress as Prince Everard wanted her to do, it wouldn't be for him. It would be for the kingdom. And wasn't that a cause noble enough to desire?

The midday meal was waiting in her room, along with a stack of books. She ate and read until the servants began to pester her about getting ready again for the evening meal. She sensed this would be a nightly event. Despite her resolutions from that morning, Isa still dreaded it, dreaded speaking with him, feeling his touch, even seeing his face. The dream of Everard and Raoul was still fresh in her mind.

But, Isa supposed, this was part of the price to pay for saving the kingdom, and for that, she would put up with it. This evening she didn't get to choose her gown. She had dawdled purposefully until it was too late for the grimy bath, and wasn't surprised when a dress of light green velvet and yellow silk was shoved at her. She endured all the shadows' pushing and pulling until she was once again handed a set of dreadful, lovely silken slippers.

"I told you," Isa folded her arms and stood firmly in place. "I'm not wearing those tonight. It's my boots or nothing." To her amazement, one of the little shadows dove furiously at her feet, nearly knocking her over. Indignation rose up inside of her. "If you think I'm going to supper without my boots, you are sorely mistaken!" she hissed. She stamped her foot down hard on the stone floor to make her point.

Isa could feel the shadows begin to swirl about her, and with a tiny bit of fear, wondered if they would continue to behave as people without bodies, or true ghosts when they were angry. Before she had too much time to worry, however, that faithful presence seemed to flood the room, and the shadows went scattering. She could feel their annoyance as they put up her hair after that, but nothing more was done about the boots.

Just moments before she was ready to walk to the dining hall, a knock sounded at her door. To her amazement, Prince Everard was waiting. He was still wearing the thick cloak, but underneath he was wearing what appeared to be a somewhat clean garment of deep brown with silver threads. It was too big for his frail body, but she had to admit that it didn't look uncomely. He looked to have washed his hair as well, as it was combed and parted neatly, the gold strands glinting in the weak light from her fireplace. He shocked her even more by giving her a stiff bow and somewhat awkwardly extending his arm.

"Good evening, Miss Isabelle. Will you allow me to escort you to supper?" Not quite sure what she was doing, Isa accepted it as if in a daze. Inwardly, she berated herself for so readily taking it, her willingness to touch the man that she loathed so. To her annoyance, she also found she wanted desperately stare into his strange fiery eyes. Though all else about him was too upsetting to look at for very long, she could have gazed into the rings of blue forever.

They walked in silence to the dining hall. Their progress was slow, and their uneven steps made scuffing sounds echo down the great stone corridors. Isa did grudgingly admit to herself that it was nice for once not to be the slow one. The man beside her was every bit as slow as she was. Somewhere in the back of her mind, she wondered what he had looked and walked like before the curse.

After the incident at the parade, Isa had avoided all events at which he'd made public appearances. Following the events, the other young women always reported with giggles that they had nearly swooned at the sight of him. How straight he stood, they would exclaim. Though he wasn't the tallest man in the court he'd carried himself powerfully, she'd heard, and that one swipe of his fist could knock a strong man unconscious. With a start, Isa realized that the prince had fallen much harder than she'd first guessed. He, who had grown up with respect and strength, was reduced to walking at the speed of a lame peasant woman. It was ironic, she thought. And yet, it brought her less satisfaction than she would have expected.

Supper was laid out by the time they arrived. Again, the prince started the conversation, his voice polite and distant.

"Were the books I sent the kind you were hoping for?"

"They . . . were satisfactory in regards to history, Your Highness."

"But?" Isa looked up from her stew to see the prince raising one of his eyebrows. He'd caught the tenor of dissatisfaction in her voice. She sighed.

"But it would be easier if I could simply browse the annals on my own." He was already shaking his head.

"That is out of the question." Isa nodded, a bit annoyed that he'd pried the request out of her when she hadn't meant to make it. He wasn't done, however. Leaning forward, he cocked his head. "Out of curiosity, why are you so intent on finding the books on your own?" Isa felt annoyance rise up in her again as she pushed her bits of meat and potatoes around the bowl.

"I need to know more about the magic." As if it weren't obvious enough.

"Magic?" He raised that eyebrow again, and Isa scoffed a bit.

"Surely you can't think that the rest of the world experiences life as . . . as you do here. In the *real* world, it's not normal for shadows to serve supper. Hundreds of life-sized statues, each as different as a man from his neighbor don't suddenly appear on a lawn and look as if they've been there for decades. It's not *normal* for doors to open on their own, or for instruments to play without musicians.

"Besides, you can't pretend all these strange things have happened only since the casting of the curse. In Soudain, even small children know the Fortress holds a special power. Whatever happened to this place came from within. I can feel it. *That* is what I need to know more about." Isa sat back and took a breath, finally glad to have gotten the chance to vent to the prince. He didn't answer immediately, but first gave her a long, shrewd look, distracting her with those strange gray and blue eyes. Finally, he answered slowly and deliberately.

"What you call *magic* does indeed exist, but there is no book in the Tower of Annals or any other place that can explain it." His eyes turned dark, and his deep voice suddenly became bitter. "It cannot be written about. It does not have that kind of nature. Many have tried, but none have succeeded, and in their frustration, they burned or destroyed what little they attempted. If you have questions, you will have to content yourself with asking me. Do you understand?" Isa nodded, a bit taken aback by the sudden storm in his voice. He'd gone from being distantly civil to a temperamental prince once again. They ate in silence until he added, more softly this time,

"I know the . . . *strength* of this Fortress better than any other creature, living or dead. What I need you to understand is that if I simply told you what you wish to find, you would never be able to break the curse. There are things you must discover for yourself before that can happen, things the Fortress will reveal to you if you need to know them." Isa stared at him, dumbfounded, as he stared sadly into night sky through the great windows behind her. She was still trying to understand what he meant when he spoke again in his polite voice.

"Are the slippers my servants chose for you not to your liking?" Isa broke out of her reverie and without thinking, looked down at her shoes. So he had noticed the boots.

"The slippers are fine," she said, "but I prefer boots." His expression was so quizzical she sighed and explained. "After the *accident*, my father had the tailor make me boots that could support my ankle. Without them, I can hardly walk, much less dance. Your servants stole my boots last night and forced me to wear the slippers." Isa's voice hitched with sudden emotion on the last words as she spoke, reminded suddenly of the last time she had tried to wear slippers at home. Gathering her resolve, she said more forcefully, "I told them that if I was to dance tonight, I would do it in my boots. I'm not about to go to bed completely lame again."

"Oh," Everard frowned in thought for a moment. "I'm sorry to hear that. I will tell them to stop bothering you about it. And . . . I'm sorry they treated you that way. They can be a bit overzealous to please sometimes." Isa nearly dropped her spoon as the apology fell from the prince's mouth. It was the last thing she had expected from the man. All she could utter was a hesitant,

"Thank you."

Before long, it was time for the dreaded dancing again. She was more prepared this time, however. The boots made her feel more confident. So did the friendly presence that followed her out onto the balcony. Isa still shuddered a bit when the prince's gloved hand held her waist, and she did not find a single moment of the awkward partnering enjoyable. But when the dancing was done, she departed feeling more like herself, feeling victorious.

The despair she'd felt the night before was gone, and this time she was more prepared to fight the memories of Raoul's dances as she returned to her room. She still had no idea as to why the prince insisted on such a strange ritual, especially when it made both of them sore, but she now knew she was capable of meeting the task.

As she turned the corner to head to her room, however, curiosity flared up inside of her. There was much Everard wasn't telling her, much she desperately needed to know if she was ever to break this curse. A reckless idea sprang to Isa's mind, and she decided to act upon it. Instead of returning to her room, she hid behind a large column until Everard had gone up the steps of the south wing.

"I'm sure you want me to break this curse as much as he does," Isa hissed at the shadows around her. "So if you dare tell him what I'm about to do, know that I will stop trying to break the curse, and you'll be stuck like this forever!" She felt the shadows' disapproval, but sensed them leaving her alone one by one.

Finally, the prince emerged. She followed him up a large winding staircase as quietly as she could. As she ascended, she passed numerous levels of halls, and down each hall were many doors that were larger than the ones in her wing of the Fortress. Isa guessed these ones led to Everard's personal chambers. She had fallen behind purposefully so he wouldn't hear her foot when it dragged, and she hoped he would be asleep soon so she could explore. Something told her that the Tower of Annals was up the dark flight of steps that led skyward from the chambers.

After a while of climbing the steps to the tower, Isa wondered if her plan had been a good one. Even in the boots, her ankle was beginning to ache from all the stairs she'd taken before she was anywhere near the top.

By the time she finally arrived, Isa had concluded that the tower she climbed must be the one that made the Fortress visible for miles. In the sunlight, it was easy to see the reflection of the glass that encircled the entire chamber. As a child, this place had stirred her curiosity and imagination. What kind of room would have only windows for walls? That curiosity was rekindled inside of her now. Remembering the prince's warning about the Tower of Annals, however, Isa restrained herself from actually entering. Instead, she knelt at the keyhole, and what she saw took her breath away.

It was larger than she'd anticipated, and it was indeed encased by windows on every side. Shelves of books filled most of the space, with the exception of the center, where there was built a large stone fireplace. The fireplace was surrounded by various chairs, tables, sofas, and even an oddly placed wardrobe. Instead of the empty room she'd expected to see, however, Everard was sitting on a low sofa with his hands stretched out before him.

Shadows gently removed the long gloves he always wore, revealing thin, gnarled fingers beneath. They were so knotted that even when he flexed them they stayed curled. Only a weak fire from a hearth and moonlight from the wall of windows lit the space, but the pain on the prince's face was obvious, and she couldn't help but pity him. Her pity didn't last long though.

Isa's gasp was nearly audible as a blue fire, much like that in his eyes, began to encircle his hands. It filled the room with a blue glow, and Everard put his head back, grimacing even harder. The scene lasted just a few seconds before the fire went out. When it was done, the prince's fingers were just a bit straighter. After curling and flexing them a few times, he slowly stood and pulled a sword from his belt, one Isa hadn't noticed beneath the cloak. Laying it down beside him, he faced the windows and slowly stretched out on a soldier's pallet. When she realized that he meant to sleep there, she turned and headed back down the stairs, not wanting to impose upon his privacy.

She struggled to sleep that night. As much as she hated to admit it, Isa couldn't be as angry with the prince as she felt she deserved to be. He'd seemed so proud when they'd met, and the hate in his eyes had been real. And yet, the pain his face was real, too. Isa knew what it felt like to go to sleep in pain. In her family, however, she had never gone to bed without a cup of tea from her mother, something to ease the pain, or a kiss from her little sister to make her feel better.

But Everard was all alone in his pain without a human hand to bring him comfort. And even when his parents were alive, Isa doubted they were the kind to spend time kissing away the hurt his childhood exploits had brought him. Suddenly, it seemed the prince, for all his splendor and power, was far more impoverished than she'd ever suspected.

And then there was the soldier's pallet. What kind of prince went to sleep with his sword, watching over his kingdom though he could hardly walk? Over and over again, Isa tried to answer the riddles the night had brought her, but the only answer that came was that perhaps, just perhaps, the prince wasn't the man she had hated for so long.

. . .

In the weeks that followed, Isa fell into a routine that wasn't altogether unpleasant. No snow had fallen since the early autumn storm her father had gotten caught in, so Isa continued her trips to the Rose garden daily. And although her ankle and wrist were broken beyond repair, as the town healer had told her when she was a child, Isa felt her body growing stronger. Each day, not only did she revel in the dance, but also in the new roses that were slowly beginning to find their way back into the garden, despite the growing cold. Moreover, it was a relief to be away from the town gossip and sympathetic looks. Here, she wasn't the town cripple. She had a purpose, strange as it may be. And though she missed her family dearly, Isa felt for the first time as if she might find a way to make them proud.

More than anything, however, Isa was grateful to have escaped Raoul's wedding. It would have been impossible to ignore if she'd still lived in Soudain. The marriage of the chancellor's only son would be the talk of the city. Their outrage at his betrayal of Isa hadn't even lasted a week after he'd broken it off with her. By the time the wedding arrived, she would have been completely forgotten, and everyone would be anxious to see the beautiful bride who had so quickly captured his heart. The wedding would come and go, and Isa was immensely grateful not to even need an excuse for her absence.

If she was honest with herself, the nightly dances still bothered her. They were too close to the moments that had been most cherished until recently. Raoul's cruel words continued to mock her as well when she let her guard slip. Nevertheless, it wasn't any worse than it had been at home.

In order to escape the lonely thoughts of her once beloved, Isa buried herself in reading the books the prince gave her. They weren't very interesting, mostly names of monarchs and dry lists of their accomplishments, but they were a distraction. And as Everard promised, his servants never made a move for her boots again. It wasn't long before a sort of truce formed between them, the prince learning how better to curb his tongue, and Isa striving to keep her tone at least civil, and sometimes kind. He even surprised her one evening by sending over a salve with his servants when he noticed that her left wrist was sore at dinner.

The presence also continued to make Isa's life at the Fortress more enjoyable. She found herself talking to it when she was lonely, telling it how much she missed her family, how Everard confused her, and on hard days, even about Raoul. She was still afraid to tell the prince about her invisible friend, fearing he might order it away. This made asking him questions about *the strength*, as he called it, even more difficult, for she knew there was some tie between the magic and her constant companion. But whenever she tried to ask, the right words wouldn't come.

Isa could sense the prince was struggling daily, not only with the physical pain she'd witnessed in the tower, but with an even deeper pain. Not wanting to upset him, the only way she could think to phrase her questions was based on the dry stories of past kings and their feats that she'd read about, but she never got very far that way. He would answer her direct questions, but never supplied any more information than was absolutely necessary. Though she was actually enjoying parts of her new life, Isa wondered how, if ever, she was to break the curse if she still had no idea as to what she was doing. It was a dark, chilly evening, a time of true winter, when things changed.

"Isabelle," the prince leaned back from his supper and gave her a mischievous grin Isa had never seen before. "That's a long name, and not terribly easy to say. Where did you get it?"

"My mother named me after the Isabelle Flower," Isa replied somewhat stiffly. Although she had secretly never loved her full name either, speaking of her mother was still difficult.

"Isabelle Flower? I've never heard of such a thing."

"It's a common miniature rose that grows in the shade," Isa explained. "I'm sure it has an official name in your Tower of Annals somewhere, but in Soudain, it's simply called the Isabelle." The prince smiled again with that boyish look and said,

"I don't think I'm going to call you Isabelle anymore. It takes too long to say. I think I'll call you Belle instead." Isa's face flushed a hot red.

"I don't–Please don't call me that, Your Highness."

"Why not?" There was no distance in his voice now, only genuine curiosity, which made it all the worse.

"I . . . ," she stuttered, searching for words as panic rose in her chest. After all this time, she'd thought she was stronger than this. "I beg your pardon, but I just don't want it!" Everard sat back and scoffed.

"I'm not asking you as the prince. I'm asking you as a fellow human who might enjoy some real conversation sometimes." Isa didn't answer, so he continued. "You've only been here for what, eight weeks? I've been here for eight months on my own. I can sense that I'm not your favorite person in the world, so believe me when I say you weren't my first choice in companions either." For some reason, that stung more than Isa would have expected. The prince continued with his cruel tirade. "Still, I've tried to get to know you, to get to you to open up just a little! But for some reason, you think you're above common civilities–"

"Civilities?" Isa snapped, and for a moment, she didn't care if she was speaking to the prince. He had crossed a line. "I didn't think it was very *civil* when you forced me here against my will, or when you made me dance with you, or when you compelled me to accept a task I *still* don't understand! What civility was there when you ended my childhood before I was ten? And even less civil was your warrant for my death last spring! *You* were the reason I was abandoned on my wedding day! You took *everything* from me! And yet, after all that *civility*, you have the gall to sit here and demand to know why I hate that name!"

The prince sat in his chair looking astonished, but Isa didn't wait for him to recover. Grabbing her mother's cloak from her chair, she threw it around her shoulders as she stomped down the steps to the nearest ground level door. She heard him yelling for her as she moved, but he wasn't fast enough to catch her.

Throwing open the door, she ran out onto the back lawn. Gusts of snowflakes were just beginning to whip furiously in the air around her, but Isa didn't care. Tears streamed down her face as she plunged headfirst toward the statues. Only after a few minutes of trudging through the accumulating snow with the frigid air penetrating her clothing did she begin to wonder where she was going. All she'd wanted to do was get away from the prince. But the snow was falling thickly, and she could not walk far in snow, even with her boots.

It didn't take her long to reach the statues, where she hoped to find some shelter from the wind before getting completely turned around. She started to breathe a sigh of relief when she reached the tall stone figures, but before she could rest, an arrow of flame fell from the sky, narrowly missing her.

With a shriek, Isa turned back toward the Fortress, but the rising snow and the stiffness of her ankle made her progress slow. More arrows followed, one of them finally catching her skirts on fire and singeing her leg. It knocked her over, but before she could even attempt to rise, a monstrous creature appeared in the sky.

It was so large, Isa could see the rings of fire in its eyes, but the fire wasn't blue like Everard's. It was gold, and it flamed brighter and brighter as the bird dove at her. Isa cried out as it struck her calf with its large beak, just above the place the arrow had scorched. Pain shot up to her thigh, and with it, the awful realization that like the creatures of the Fortress, this bird was no typical bird of prey. The hawk made a large arc over her in the sky, and had turned to dive at her again when a sword was suddenly thrust between the fowl and its prey.

Isa turned to see Everard's hunched form standing above her. He shook with the effort to keep the sword raised so high, but the hawk was stopped before it could finish its plunge.

"Go!" he ordered. Isa scrambled to stand, wincing at the burning in her leg, and together, they headed back toward the castle. They moved sluggishly, however, and though the prince kept his sword raised, the bird regained its confidence and began to strike at them once more. Over and over it struck, but it didn't touch her again.

By the time they made it back, Isa was more exhausted and frightened than she'd ever been in her life. The pain in her leg was agonizing. Her alarm grew even greater when she turned to look at Everard. His neck, arms, and face were covered in gashes. He nearly dropped his sword to the floor when the door was shut, but instead of collapsing, he gripped her arm and dragged her to the nearest chair. Wordlessly, Isa let him. Shadows rushed around to feed the nearest fireplace.

"Pull up your dress," he barked. Shocked, Isa stared at him. "If I don't tend to your leg, you will lose it! Would you like that?" he bellowed at her. Still unable to speak, Isa shook her head and slowly lifted her gown up to her knee. The flesh on her shin was shiny and red, and as soon as she saw it, the pain was nearly unbearable. Above the burn was a large gash from which blood was dripping down. The sight made her suddenly very dizzy, and it took all of Isa's strength not to faint.

To distract herself, she tried to focus on Everard's eyes. He had stiffly dropped to his knees, and was yelling out orders to the servants, calling for herbs and bandages. It was only then that she recalled his warning from her first evening there, telling her never to leave the Fortress at night. Guilt settled over her as she continued to stare into her prince's eyes.

His face was pale and flushed at the same time from the effort he'd just exerted. Beads of sweat ran down his temples, making lines in the dirt and soot that covered his face. The blue fire in his eyes was blazing more brightly than she'd ever seen it, and with a start, she realized the presence that had followed her around for the past weeks was in him as well. She suddenly understood that it was the presence itself from which his strength was derived. So the presence wasn't a stranger to him either.

Seeing him there, covered in blood and soot, nearly weak enough to pass out himself and yet tending to her wound, Isa's stomach did a strange flop. By that time, the servants had surrounded them with all sorts of herbs, salves, water, and bandages. When he removed his gloves, his claw-like hands were shaking, but he somehow still moved more quickly than she'd ever seen him. He expertly mixed the herbs and rubbed them on her wound.

"What were you thinking?" His voice was low and dangerous.

"I . . . I'm sorry," Isa whispered.

"Do you not remember me specifically telling you to stay inside at night?" he exploded. Isa could only stare at him with sorrowful eyes. "You were nearly killed out there! You don't seem to comprehend what your life is no longer your own! You're still under the delusion that what you do only affects you! Let me put this simply. If you die, I don't stand a chance at restoring the Fortress or the kingdom! Think about that next time you're of the mind to do something foolish!"

"I'm sorry," Isa whispered again. And she was. If it hadn't been for her infernal temper, neither of them would be bleeding right now. He might have been cruel, but it was she who had lost self-control and foolishly run out into the storm. She should have been stronger than that. The prince took a deep breath and stopped working.

"I'm sorry, Isabelle. My words aren't meant to hurt you. I'm frustrated because I should have been better able to protect you." In that moment, Isa saw a flash of the warrior he had once been, and it was obvious that his current weakness shamed him greatly. "You don't know what it's like to be a soldier, to stand guard at the gates of evil, to know without a doubt that you can overcome it . . . and then to have all that stripped away, to be forced to watch as your kingdom slowly burns to the ground."

An awkward quiet settled over them for what felt like an eternity. Finally, Isa could stand the silence no more.

"You are quite skilled with wounds." The prince didn't look up as he carefully wrapped her leg in a white cloth.

"Rarely in battle is there a healer around when he's needed. All of my men are required to learn the basic healing skills. If they don't, many soldiers die."

"Who were they, the people that attacked us?" Isa tried to quiet her hammering heart, but fear still consumed her. He didn't answer until he'd finished wrapping her leg and his gloves were back on. Finally, he looked her in the eyes. There was no playfulness there this time, no spite, nothing but an earnest frustration. He measured her for a long moment before saying,

"Come with me. There's something you need to see." Isa wasn't sure she would be able to walk, but as soon as she stood up, she could feel the expertise of the prince's work. There was hardly any pain aside from the usual ache of her ankle as she followed him to the stairs she'd snuck up once before.

"What you are about to see has only ever been seen by the Fortress kings and queens and their closest confidantes. It's sacred, the heart of the Fortress. But," he turned to her with that strange contemplative look, "if you can truly break the curse, it will affect more than just this Fortress and its inhabitants. What happens in this room will one day determine the fate of our world and our enemies."

When they finally reached the top of the tower, Isa could see sweat still trickling down the prince's neck in the weak torchlight. She was breathing hard herself from the effort of the long climb. When he unlocked the door, however, the view made her forget the exhaustion. She gasped as she stepped into the tower of windows. He led her over to the north side of the room. From there, she could see a great encampment at the foot of the mountain. Despite the dark, hundreds of fires lit up the night. They made it easy to see the countless rows of tents that stood tauntingly.

"You can't see them from your room," he said quietly. "I put you there on purpose so you couldn't, but that is the enemy."

"Who are they? What are they waiting for?" Her heart began to thump unevenly again.

"In the thousand years this Fortress has stood, it has never gone dark. Tonight's attack was a warning, a taunt. They're reminding me that they're watching."

"Why do they hate you so much?" Isa turned to look at him.

"The Fortress isn't the only source of power and strength in the world." He stared out at the enemy, his eyes troubled. "And yet, Destin is different from all of the other kingdoms. For a thousand years, it has been the strongest of all. What did you learn of the first king, Cassiel, in your reading?" Isa racked her memory, running quickly through the dozens of droll histories she'd been reading.

"Wasn't he once a knight for another kingdom?" Everard nodded.

"He was a low-ranking knight of a nearby land, a man of little consequence. He entered the lower country of his land, what's now Soudain, and saw the injustices being inflicted upon the people because of his proud king's negligence. The Maker's hand was upon Cassiel as he set out to right the wrongs evil had brought that the nobles of his land ignored. He turned a barren wasteland full of impoverished souls into a safe and prosperous haven. As a result, the people there were blessed with rich soil and flowing streams.

"In addition, the Maker gifted him with the Fortress, a place from which he could draw a special strength to do justice and provide mercy. That strength was passed on to his descendants as well. That is why the Fortress is more than just a castle, a pile of rocks and mortar. It's been a place of light and hope for a millennium. Until now."

"How is it then that this . . . strength is disappearing so quickly? If the Fortress was created with such power, how can they attack us so ruthlessly, particularly at night?" Isa couldn't tear her eyes away from the fires below.

"There are other powers that wander this earth," Everard frowned. "They have never been able to match the strength given this place, but that doesn't mean they should ever be underestimated. Our greatest enemy, Tumen, has been a source of dark power for hundreds of years, a thorn in our side." Turning from the window, the prince shook his head in disgust and sank into a chair.

"Not long before he died, my father sought an alliance with Tumen. My betrothal ball put an end to that, however, thanks to the true intentions of their princess and some ill-chosen words on my part." The idea of Everard having a betrothal ball was somewhat troublesome to Isa for some reason, but she ignored it and asked a more appropriate question.

"I still don't understand where their power comes from. How were they able to hit me so well through the snowstorm? To see me even? And why would they attack only at night? Surely it would be easier by day."

"Greed is a powerful weapon of its own," The prince gave a strange, hard smile. "Cultivated and nourished enough, it can be twisted into an asset of surprising force. King Cassiel was born in Tumen, and served its king until he left to right the injustices he found here. Tumen always believed that because Cassiel was one of its own knights, Soudain rightfully belonged to the Tumen king. Their rage at being denied sovereignty of this land became their weapon. The Tumenian power is nearly as old as that of the Fortress, only it is one shrouded in evil. It cannot stand the light of day.

"Princess Nevina, until recently, was the declared heir of Tumen's throne. When she was small, her father trained her in the ways of their ancestors. She proved to be strong, and many believed she would be the one to restore Soudain to them. It has long made them unpopular with the other kingdoms, and while the Tumenian king claims to have given up his dark powers in order to seek peace, Nevina never had any such intentions. The birth of a son took the kingdom by surprise, however, and Nevina lost her claim to the throne."

"So the princess is allowed to run about doing whatever she wishes now?"

"Her people have always loved her, and Nevina is clever. She's using their affection to garner support, and has continued to grow her numbers with her promises of the richness of our land. And for all his claims of peace, her father has done nothing to stop her." Everard shook his head, his next words taking Isa by surprise.

"I fear, however, that her greed is not the power that has threatened this kingdom most in these last generations. She's merely taken advantage of what we've been giving her." Isa waited for him to go on, but he didn't, suddenly lost in his own revelations. It was a moment before he spoke again.

"We've been able to hold Tumen off for centuries. With each generation, however, they've grown stronger. My father, his father, and even his father did everything they could to ensure our allies' loyalties and to minimize Destin's weaknesses. But the more we've tried, the harder it's become. And now they wait." As she pondered his words and watched his eyes, Isa had a sudden flash of insight.

"The curse didn't just affect your body. You're losing your power, too, aren't you?" His eyes once again flaming a duller fire, Everard smiled wryly.

"The strength that has flowed through the blood of my ancestors has been diminishing for generations. It seems my line is no longer fit to bear the burden anymore. At least, not until this curse is broken."

Isa finally understood his desperation to break the curse. The prince, like her, hungered to fulfill his purpose. Everyone knew King Rodrigue had raised his son to be a warrior prince to protect Destin. And yet, after all he'd done, everything he'd tried to do, it still wasn't enough. He was losing everything that he'd ever held dear, and as much as she wanted to blame him, Isa was slowly having to admit that perhaps a stronger force was at work in their lives, one that not even the great prince had control over.

And it was breaking him, as it had broken her. Isa fought the sudden desire to reach out and touch him, to embrace him and tell him everything would be alright. Instead, she kept her hands firmly in her lap and decided to answer his question from earlier that evening.

"It's not your fault I hate the name Belle," she said softly. Everard turned from staring at the fires again to look at her, his open expression suddenly making him look very young. Isa tried not to get trapped in his gaze. "I was engaged," her voice quivered, the pain resurfacing as she spoke. "His name is Raoul. He was always there for me, since childhood. After the injury, I felt very alone. The other children didn't want to wait for the crippled girl to constantly catch up, and he was the only one who still saw me for me. He would come over and play with me when I couldn't leave the house, and he would bring me things that made me smile, like flowers from a field or apples from an orchard we used to explore.

"As we got older," Isa smiled at the memory in spite of herself, "he was the only one who ever asked me to dance. He called me Belle because," Isa's voice caught, and she had to whisper so she wouldn't cry, "he said I was the hidden flower, the one that was too beautiful for everyone to see." Despite her resolve, warm tears coursed silently down her cheeks as she spoke.

"What happened?" When Isa looked up at him, the prince's face was full of what looked like sincere concern. Isa's hand went to her crooked wrist without thinking.

"He proposed to me just after the Fortress went dark, then left immediately with his father on a long journey. His father is the city chancellor, and has been preparing his son for the position since he was born. Apparently, he wanted Raoul to see what a *true* leader's wife should look like." Isa's voice hitched again, and instead of stopping, her tears fell harder. The shame of the memory made Isa's face hot. "He returned on our wedding day. He told me . . . He made it very clear that I was unfit to be the wife of a chancellor, that my weaknesses made me unable to fulfill the role being his wife would require. I wasn't enough."

Unable to hold in the sobs, Isa put her head in her hands and wept. The pain of being broken was much fresher than she thought it would be by now. Raoul had broken her again just when she thought she was about to be healed. It felt as if she would never be whole again. This shame and sorrow of not being enough would follow her forever.

It was a few moments before she was calm enough to look into the eyes of her prince, and suddenly, she felt humiliated. What foolishness had possessed her to think he cared or wanted to know her pathetic love story? He had greater concerns on his mind. When she was finally brave enough to steal a glance at him, however, Everard's face looked like one of the stone statues that stood outside. His jaw was set tightly, and the blue in his eyes blazed brightly once more. She was a bit frightened at first until she realized he wasn't angry at her. He said nothing as he walked over to the window again and stared down at the enemy below.

"My family calls me Isa," she finally volunteered.

"And my friends call me Ever," he answered solemnly. Isa couldn't help but wonder if she was supposed to call him this, too. Was she now considered a friend? As she puzzled over this, he quietly added, "For what it's worth, I still think Belle fits you better." In a daze, Isa simply gazed up at him. Silence settled over them again, the fire's crackling making the only sounds as the evening drew late.

"You should go to bed soon," he finally said in a rough voice. Isa knew he was right, but her eyes wandered back to the campfires below. Fear rushed through her every time she looked at them. "You don't have to be afraid," the prince was now looking at her with a gentleness she'd never seen before on his face. "They've been here for months. They won't attack again tonight." Isa nodded, but her eyes stayed locked on the fires below, her leg beginning to throb where the bird had slashed it.

Without warning, Everard began to sing. Isa knew none of the words. They seemed as ancient as the Fortress which surrounded her, but the incredibly rich tones of the prince's voice conveyed the meaning just as easily as if she'd spoken the language.

Gentle one who shivers with fear
Tremble no more in your fright
One who is stronger watches over you
No harm shall meet thee tonight.

As if under a spell, Isa found herself dozing off against the arm of the chair she sat in. She was vaguely aware of airy hands lifting her, floating her to her chambers on a breeze. She didn't dream of Raoul that night, or even the flaming arrows. Instead, Ever's rich voice serenaded her to a place of peace and rest, and it was with a smile on her face that Isa fell asleep.

CHAPTER 10

"Garin," Ever crumpled into a chair near the fire, his shadow servants scrambling to tend to his spent and bloody body. "I need something to drink, something that will clear my head." A few moments later, a shadow figure handed him a goblet filled with a putrid brown liquid. Ever usually would have stared at it and then peppered Garin with a dozen questions as to what it was, but tonight he was too shaken to do anything but gulp it down.

He hadn't meant to tell her so much. He hadn't meant for any of it to happen. The jesting about her name had simply been a foolish attempt at lightening the mood, an attempt to reach past the walls she had built around herself. He'd had no idea it would affect her the way it had.

Shame and fury raced through his veins as he recalled the frustration of trying to race after her, to protect her. As she'd run into the darkness, his instincts had kicked in, but his body had not been able to keep up. It was as if someone was holding him back, as if chains had been tied to his legs as he tried desperately to reach the one person who might be able to unlock the Fortress's secrets for him. He knew deep down, however, that there was something else that had drawn him after her so quickly as well.

Isabelle . . . *Isa* fascinated him. She wasn't like any other woman he'd ever met. The court girls who threw themselves after him were generally silly, witless creatures who were about as deep as a puddle. And though he suspected there were wiser women in the court, they had tended to avoid him.

His hands still shook as he finished off the last drops of Garin's awful drink. His head was clearing, but that was ultimately making him feel worse. The more he thought about Isa's story, the angrier he became with the weak coward who had broken her heart. Even worse, he knew that his treatment of her was no better. The weasel who had dared to break off their engagement on the night of her wedding had traded the young woman for power. Ever knew he was truly no better, trying to gain her affections to reach the same end. And no matter how many times he tried to justify her sacrifice with the needs of the kingdom, it all came down to one thing. He was undeniably using her. And it didn't help matters now that his heart was inexplicably tangled up in the matter as well.

At first, the chivalry had been purely an act. He'd gritted his teeth every time he offered his arm to the woman with the dark blue eyes who had haunted his dreams for so long. The guilt of what he'd done to her had fueled his rage at first, and it had taken all of his acting skills, those he'd practiced for dealing with untrustworthy diplomats and dignitaries, to keep the sneer from his face.

But there was something disarming about her. From her willingness to sacrifice herself for her family to her determination to dance, he'd quickly found himself more perplexed with her than anything else. How he wanted to draw the secrets from those eyes. He hadn't dared to admit his obsession even to himself, however, until he'd seen her on the ground, bleeding into the snow.

Something had changed as he tried to charge toward her. If he'd been in his old body, she would never have even seen the arrow, for he would have had her back in the Fortress before she'd reached the statues. A type of alien anxiety had filled him as he watched her cry out into the night, the pain and fear all over her face. The same helplessness had filled him as she broke down, recalling the way her fiancé had abandoned her. Ever didn't sleep that night. Instead, he stared down at the campfires below until the break of dawn.

. . .

Isa didn't dance the next day. Ever made sure of that. He ordered his servants to keep her in bed and tend to her leg no matter what kind of fight she put up.

"You could heal her, Sire," Garin had suggested gently. Ever shook his head.

"I can't spend any strength that's not absolutely necessary. With the proper care, she'll heal on her own." Deep down, however, guilt ate at him, as he knew he was being selfish. Not only was he hoarding the strength he had once spent easily on himself, but he was also planning on using her required bed rest as an excuse to visit her in a place where she couldn't escape his attention.

"Garin, I'd like you to come with me this morning to learn what she thinks of me," Ever announced as his servants helped him to dress. Garin gave a polite snort.

"Your Highness, I can tell you that now. She has absolutely no idea what she thinks about you. But you know I'll be there with you as I always am."

The visit was somewhat awkward. Ever thought about bringing flowers, but as the only live ones on the Fortress grounds were in Isa's beloved rose garden, he decided against it. Instead, he brought more books. She politely greeted him from bed when he knocked. Ever grinned to himself as the female shadows flitted about angrily when he entered. He knew they didn't think it proper for the prince to visit a woman in her bedchambers, but they settled down somewhat when Garin floated in behind him.

After sharing such deep emotions the night before, neither Isa nor Ever knew quite what to say, but the air between them was most assuredly altered. It didn't help either that Ever found himself continually distracted by the way her wavy auburn hair framed her heart-shaped face. The servants had left it down since she was in bed, and it was a surprising length. It gave her a softer appearance, making her look more vulnerable than he'd ever seen. Multiple times, he caught himself wondering what it would feel like to touch her face.

By the end of the visit, not much had been really said between the two humans in the room, but Ever could hear Garin smothering his chuckles, and realized the female servants were very ready to shoo him out. Apparently, his thoughts hadn't been as well hidden as he'd believed them to be.

The days that followed weren't any less awkward. Thanks to Ever's quick binding skills, Isa's leg was healed within a few weeks. Ever felt a bit bad about this. He knew that if he really wanted to, he could heal her using his strength. If she suspected his selfishness, however, she gave nothing away. Instead, their relationship seemed to improve. While they were not exactly friends, Ever found that she no longer sent him scathing looks over her supper, and she stopped trembling when he led her to the dance floor each night. While she was far from throwing herself at him, it seemed at least her hatred of him had subsided.

And if Isa's actions didn't confuse him enough, Ever's emotions did the job.

"You must guard yourself, Son," Rodrigue had told Ever after his first ball. The poor boy had been dumbstruck by the great number of eligible beauties that had paraded themselves in front of the young prince that night, hoping to capture his attention before he was old enough to make a decision. "A worthy woman will bear a king children, but she will easily become a distraction as well. You must protect this kingdom before all else, and that includes your queen."

King Rodrigue had lived by his word. Queen Louise rarely saw her husband. Rumor had it that the king had all but stopped visiting the queen's chambers once Ever was born. Always training the soldiers, always on a campaign, and forever consulting with his generals, Rodrigue believed his marital duties had been fulfilled when his wife produced a son. Just as he abstained from all strong drink and any food that might be considered gluttonous, just as he slept keeping watch from the sacred Tower of Annals, he'd denied himself the company of a woman all in the name of duty.

Ever had tried to follow his father's instructions, but just as the idea of picking a wife based on politics alone had made him apprehensive, ignoring the draw he now felt to Isa seemed impossible. Finally, tired of being at war with his logic and his desires, he called Garin.

"Have you discovered something that will win her affections?"

"Do you mean something that will win her heart, or something that will hasten your plan?" Ever rolled his eyes.

"I don't see what difference it makes," he snapped. "If the plan is going to work, she might as well be happy about it." Despite the steward's shadowy appearance, Ever could just imagine Garin's mouth turning down at one corner and the thin wrinkles around his eyes deepening as they always did when he didn't approve of something. But he responded,

"As for the plan, you can see for yourself that the crystal glows brighter with each night," he said. "As for earning her love, she no longer despises you, if that's what you're asking." Ever gave a short laugh.

"While I'd agree that's a start, I'm asking what I should do next. I've never–I don't even know where to start." Ever walked out onto the tower's balcony. A breeze ruffled his left sleeve as Garin came to stand beside him. The air was warmer today than it had been for a long time. Spring was on its way.

"No man has ever truly mastered the way to a woman's heart," Garin's voice was kinder this time. "And anyone who thinks he has doesn't deserve her." They were silent for a moment as the sound of a lone jay was carried to them on the wind. It had been a long time since any bird had dared to makes its home on the Fortress grounds. In spite of his misgivings, Ever found a small shred of hope in the lonely sound.

"You know about the old way of choosing a queen on the crystal balcony," Garin said softly. "When one of the women brought a fire of her own to make the crystal glow, it meant the Fortress had chosen her as its queen. There is something your father never told you though, probably because his father never told him. It's true that the young ladies would present themselves to the future king, and it's also true that they would dance on the crystal floor until one showed a sufficient strength of her own, just as you're attempting to do with Isa.

"But the kings of old didn't stop there. You see, any king could find a woman of worth by looking for an answer from the crystal floor, but a wise king did not stop there. He would realize the Fortress had chosen for him a jewel, a pillar of strength to be his helper, his partner in guarding Destin." Ever could hear the smile in his mentor's voice as he spoke.

"In the stories you begged me to tell when you were little, the queens weren't treated as delicate flowers to be left in their chambers, produce children, and amuse themselves. They were advisers to their husbands, and their words were regarded more highly than generals', for the wise kings trusted that the Fortress had chosen for them only the best. A number of the great queens even learned to wield the strength just as well, if not better, than their husbands could."

"What happened?" Ever frowned as he took this all in. He'd always prided himself in knowing the history of the Fortress. How had he not known this?

"The kings stopped trusting the Fortress, to put it simply," Garin suddenly sounded tired. "They believed they knew best, and as a result, the queens were chosen for alliances and politics, rather than virtue and strength. With all due respect to your mother, of course, the bright lights that burned by the kings' sides disappeared."

"While that's all quite interesting," Ever shook his head to clear it and turned to go back inside. It was nearly time for his daily ride, something he insisted on continuing as long as he was physically able. "I don't see how that's going to help me with Isa."

"It's really quite simple, Your Highness," Garin said after calling for two shadow servants to prepare the prince's riding things. "If you saw a jewel buried in the dirt, what would you do?"

"I'd pick it up."

"But you wouldn't just pick it up, would you? You'd lift if gently. You'd take your time so as not to scratch it. And once you had it in your hands, you wouldn't allow it to stay filthy. You would make it shine. You would brush the dirt off, polish it. And the more you worked, the brighter it would shine."

"Garin, please, I didn't sleep last night, and my mind is not up to answering your riddles."

"Everard, Isa is the jewel, one that has been drawn to the Fortress just as the queens of old were. Just as a jewel needs someone to help it shine, so does this woman. Heartbreak isn't easy to clean up. Lift her up, make her see her worth, and she might surprise you with her brilliance." By this time, they were on their way down to the stables. Once they were there, Ever painfully pulled himself up onto his horse. He kicked the animal into a quick canter, but he could hear Garin call out from behind him, "The Fortress has brought her to you for a reason, Ever! You might want to reconsider trusting it to help both of you break the curse!"

Ever didn't answer as he rode quickly toward the north end of the Fortress grounds. His joints ached with each of the horse's steps, but riding was the only way he could move fast enough to think to his satisfaction. As he made his way toward the northern edge of the Fortress grounds, however, he suddenly felt as if he was being watched. Sure enough, when he turned around, a large pair of dark eyes were following him from the grand entrance where Isa stood in the doorway. She looked nervous. Ever's curiosity got the best of him, and he cut his ride short. His father would have been appalled.

"Can I help you, my lady?" he called out, somewhat shocked at his confidence as the words left his mouth. Isa gave him a half smile.

"I would like to go out, but I'm not sure if the weather agrees with me." Ever noticed the catch in her voice, however, and saw right through her brave face. He brought his horse right up to the grand doors, still held open by the shadows as Isa lingered on the threshold.

"There's nothing to be afraid of." As he spoke, he realized he sounded like a commander insulting one of his cowardly soldiers. "Remember, the danger is only at night. Their birds and archers can't see well until the sun has set." Why was it so hard to soften his voice? Isa smiled, but he could still see her trembling hands. Suddenly wondering if he could do as Garin had advised, he stiffly dismounted and held his arm out to her. "Would you like me to accompany you to the garden?"

The young woman studied him for a moment, tilting her head a bit as she stared at him with those dark eyes. Ever wasn't sure what she saw there, but she finally nodded lightly and took his arm. Together, they shuffled down the stone path to the rose garden. For the first time since the curse had fallen, Ever didn't mind the slow pace. The warmth of her arm felt nice on his, and the soft skin of her right hand as it gently grasped his arm made his heart jump unevenly. She kept her head down, staring at the ground as they walked, but Ever longed to lift her chin so she would look him in the eyes. Though he escorted her to supper every night, this felt different, more intimate outside in the thin sunlight that was almost warm. For all his father's training in self-denial and duty, he felt like an adolescent again. With a bit of disgust, he realized his constantly growing desire to be near her was somewhat akin to that of a puppy.

"Would you mind if we go somewhere else today?" he asked as they approached the rose garden, suddenly desperate to keep her arm and her attention. Isa turned to him with wide eyes.

"Where would you like to go?" Ever honestly had no idea. He said the first thing that came to mind.

"If you're going to live here, you might as well know a bit about the grounds. They weren't always as they are now." Isa's eyes stayed wide, as if this was the last thing she'd expected, but to his relief, she nodded. And so they began to explore the many gardens that had once adorned the Fortress's front lawns. Ever pointed out places in the foliage and shrubs where he'd played as a child. As he told her stories of how he'd evaded his tutors and hidden with the servant children, Isa seemed to relax. She even laughed a few times when he mentioned some particularly ornery tricks he'd played on Garin.

"You really love this place," Isa said as they stopped to rest on a stone bench in the ancient Garden of the Queens.

"I was born with a love for this place," Ever answered uncomfortably. "As a child, I never felt alone. Even when I escaped to be on my own, I always felt loved and protected. It was as if the Fortress itself had wrapped its arms around me. I felt special."

"But you don't feel that way now?" Ever sighed. Isa's guesses were getting better, and she was fast approaching a conversation he preferred not even to have with himself.

"I used to know how I felt. I knew what the Fortress was doing. It was a part of me. But ever since this curse, since this sickness has fallen, I've felt alone." He let out a gusty breath. "To be honest, the Fortress has abandoned me. Garin always told me the Fortress never abandoned anyone it chose, but I can't say I believe that anymore."

"Oh," Isa was quiet for a few moments. Ever watched her out of the corner of his eye. She stared at her left wrist, turning it over again and again in her lap, tracing out the lines in her skin with her other hand. As she did, Ever suddenly found himself staring at her lips. They looked soft, and he resisted the sudden urge to touch them. Before his thoughts could wander further, however, Isa spoke again. "Garin seems wise. At least, I always thought so."

"You can hear Garin, too?" Ever froze. Was she that strong already? But Isa shook her head with a small smile on those soft lips.

"No, but I knew him as a child. He and my father were friends. He was always kind to me." She leaned toward him just a bit, a sudden curiosity in her eyes. "The last time I saw him was when he was in town a year ago, before the Fortress went dark. He didn't look as if he'd aged a bit since the day I first met him!" Her voice fell to an excited whisper. "What exactly *is* he?" Ever chuckled.

"Honestly? A mystery. He's been the steward here for as long as I've been alive, and I believe as long as my father was alive as well. In fact, there's no one here who can remember a time when Garin wasn't here. Believe me, I've asked *everyone*. He's just as much a part of the Fortress as the walls and the tapestries."

"If that's true, he must have some of that . . . What did you call it? Strength. He must have some of that strength, too, right?"

"Yes and no," Ever picked up a stick and began to idly draw with it in the gravel at his feet. "While he doesn't wield the strength of the Fortress the way the monarchs do, he has a strange resistance to the powers of our dark enemies. It's as if the monarchs were placed here to guard the Fortress and the kingdom, and Garin was placed here to guard the monarchs. He guarded me, at least," Ever recalled solemnly. "If it hadn't been for Garin, I might have grown up devoid of affections completely." Isa watched him with curious eyes. It felt empowering to have her look at him without anger or fear.

"So you didn't see your parents often?" Ever snorted, hearing the questions she was really asking.

"My father was rarely around, and when he was, he was either training his troops for battle or preparing me for the life of a soldier. My mother loved parties and balls, and rarely had time for anything else. I went through a series of governesses as a child, largely because I wore most of them out before they had time to acclimate to palace life. Garin and the servants were the ones who watched out for me, and it was only because of them that I knew anyone else had a family that was more closely knit than mine."

"I see," Isa thought for a moment before a small smile grew on her face and a slight blush colored her cheeks. "I doubt you were that hard to love as a child."

"And how would you know that?" Ever let out a laugh. Her smile widened.

"When I would accompany my father here to do business, I would sometimes watch you from afar." Ever felt like his heart might beat out of his chest, but he swallowed and tried to keep his voice even.

"And what did you think?" Isa gave a little laugh and leaned back, closing her eyes as the sun moved out from behind the clouds. Ever didn't even pretend to look away this time, staring as rudely as it was possible for a gentleman to do. But she had him truly curious. And her smile was lovely.

"I thought you seemed kind, different from you father. Not that he was unkind," she hastened to say. "But you talked to the servants as if they were friends. I think you even spotted me staring once, while you were heading out for a riding lesson." Her face fell, however, as she reminisced. Guilt and shame flooded him as Ever realized the direction of her thoughts. He wanted to fall on the ground suddenly, to beg for her forgiveness, but he couldn't get his feet to move. Instead, he closed his eyes.

"I know my words now can never make up for what I did to you. I won't attempt to excuse my actions either. But," he took a deep breath, "I need you to know that I wasn't the monster you must have thought me for so many years, not even the monster I am now. I was a boy who was struggling to be someone he wasn't." Isa was silent, and he was terrified to look at her, so he continued in a rush.

"The memory of your face has haunted me for years, the way you looked at me when you fell. You changed me that day. You showed me what evil I was capable of if I didn't learn to control my strength. But I couldn't accept it. It was too much to bear to realize that I *could* be a beast. It was easier to hate you instead." Finally, he drew his eyes up to meet hers. They were guarded, her lips parting slightly as she considered his words.

"Please," he whispered, "know that I wasn't always as I am today. Know that I'm sorrier than I can ever express." Her eyes stayed wary, and her hands shook a bit as they clutched her skirts tightly. But she uttered the most beautiful words he'd ever heard.

"I believe you."

They walked back to the Fortress in silence after that, not even speaking a word when they parted. Too tired to resume his ride, Ever went to the stables and simply sat next to his horse. The day had certainly not turned out the way he'd expected. But as much as he hated to admit it, Garin had been right, at least about Isa. It had taken a long time for Isa to look at, much less speak to him with any level of confidence or closeness. He just hoped it wouldn't take too much longer for her to move beyond mere warmth. His strength was still waning quickly, and there wasn't much time left.

As spring drew nearer and Ever's strength did indeed dwindle, Isa's grew visibly by the day. It wasn't long before the rose garden was fairly glowing with its brilliant blooms of not only pink, but also red, yellow, peach, white, violet, and even blue. The snow melted and was not replaced. Ever might have attributed it to the cycles of nature if it hadn't been that Isa's favorite paths were always the ones to return far before the others. When he went to escort her to supper one evening, Ever couldn't help but notice the smell of fresh vanilla in the halls of the northern wing near Isa's room. Nostalgia and panic hit him as he recalled that before the curse, Gigi had always placed sprigs of the plant all over the Fortress. It seemed now that she was doing it again. The dark, wet stones in the walls and the floors began to slowly regain their white marble swirls, and dust and dirt no longer covered every surface.

The gradual lifting of the curse was undeniable, however, the day Ever heard a shriek from Isa's room. A strange dread filled him as he did his best to race toward her, pushing himself so fast he nearly tripped down the stairs of the tower to get to her. After a long and painful trek down many halls, he arrived, breathless, to find Isa's door open. Rushing in, he stopped short to see Isa and one of the servant women laughing and hugging one another, happy tears running down their faces. The servant was the first to spot him, and pulling herself from Isa's embrace, bowed low.

"Your Highness!" Ever looked in shock from one woman to the other.

"Ever," Isa's smile was brighter than any he'd ever seen on her face. She was glowing with elation. "This is Cerise! She and I were good friends when we were children!" After pulling her friend back into another hug, Isa asked him, "But how can it be? What brought her back?" It took all of Ever's self-control to attempt an even answer.

"Your strength must be growing." Isa's face changed to one of amazement.

"I have strength? You mean, the kind that you do?"

"It would seem so," was all Ever could say before turning and storming out of the room. He could see the confusion in Isa's eyes at his hasty and rather rude departure, but as he walked back down the hall, he could hear the two women laughing and talking again. This was all wrong. He knew he should be happy. He'd been right all along. Isa *was* the key to freeing the Fortress from its curse.

But her power was supposed to include healing *him*, he thought with confusion. He'd noticed the servants' shadows growing thicker in the recent weeks, and there were other signs like the return of the birds and the green of the gardens. But as the Fortress was loosed from the darkness that had held it captive and alone for the last year, Ever continued to grow weaker.

He tried to understand what had gone wrong. He'd heard Isa talking to the Fortress when she thought he couldn't hear her, which meant she'd discovered its presence unaided, the presence that had abandoned him. It was a presence very few people could sense. Not even his father had been able to feel it as she seemed to. She already had a strength greater than many of the kings, it appeared, and she wasn't even aware of it. She was healing everything around her without effort. Everything but him.

For the first time in a long time, Ever wondered if his plan would truly work. Even if he did marry her, would she be able to heal him? The Fortress was indeed preparing her for something great, but it seemed to be excluding him. Anger gathered in the pit of Ever's stomach. The Fortress had betrayed him, and worse, had brought in a stranger to replace him. Even more cruel, the woman it brought was the one woman in the world he'd ever found irresistible. This anger made Ever even more determined to carry out his plan. She would soon be ready to become a keeper of the Fortress. He would marry her, she would heal him, and all would be restored. His duty would go on. It just had to.

Preparing for supper was difficult for Ever that night. Resentment for Isa filled his heart as he shuffled down the hall to escort her to the dining hall. And yet, when Isa answered his knock that night, he felt his breath leave him.

She had always been lovely, but tonight, she looked every part a princess. Her blue eyes sparkled with excitement, and her cheeks were faintly flushed with color. The joy in her smile was dazzling. For the first time, she no longer looked like a stranger in her own body, a terrified doe ready to duck at the first sign of danger. Tonight, she stood as erectly as her ankle would allow her, and she smiled with confidence. It was perhaps the confidence that allowed all the rest to shine. And as much as Ever resented her growing power, he couldn't help but gawk at the young woman who stood before him now.

For once, Isa didn't stop talking that night. She had endless questions about what had happened with Cerise, and Ever found himself at a loss for words, something he wasn't accustomed to. He kept getting lost in his own thoughts as he stared at her. Confusion stirred within him, feelings he couldn't put a name to. Years of nothing but war and his father's ever watchful eye had kept his eyes averted from women, and now it was as if he'd never seen one before. His bitterness and admiration for her and the guilt for how he was using her all warred within him.

"You haven't heard a word I've said, have you?" Isa wore a bemused smile. Ever smiled politely in return.

"I apologize. I've had much on my mind today."

"Why are you doing that?" She suddenly leaned forward and rested her chin on her right fist.

"Doing what?"

"Treating me differently, like a lady?" Because he'd made it very clear in the beginning that she was his servant, a captive in this hell of a prison. Ever paused before answering. It was hard for him to find words for the torrents of emotions and desires that suddenly raged inside of him, and he wasn't sure he really wanted to.

"Isa, I know I wasn't the perfect gentleman when you arrived, far from it." He stood stiffly and went to stare into the night sky out the great window behind her. "I used to think I knew what I was doing at all times. Rules and regulations made sense. You do what you're told and the world moves along rightly. But this," he gestured at the dining hall with a sweep of his arm, "I'm not accustomed to this kind of living. I don't have rules to follow, and I don't have words to speak.

"I'm trying," he turned pleading eyes upon her, begging her silently for forgiveness for a sin she didn't know he was committing even now as he spoke. "I want to be a good man, but sometimes I fear there's not enough grace in the world to make me into that man." Isa stared at him silently. How he wanted to know what she was thinking behind those eyes. Would she be able to forgive him if she found out how he was trying to use her?

"I think you're a good man." Her voice was nearly inaudible. "I just think . . . ." Then, as if she suddenly remembered his station, she shook her head and lowered her eyes to the floor. "I'm sorry. It's not my place to judge."

"No, I want to hear," Ever returned to the table.

"I think you've just lost your way. I think you've forgotten the simple goodness of this place, the goodness you knew as a child. Not that I know much of war, but it seems like your father's pursuit of it, if I may say so, was more than a simple desire to protect Destin. Sometimes we can get so caught up in protecting ourselves that we forget to see what's truly before us."

A thoughtful look filled Isa's eyes as she stared into the fireplace. "But the longer I'm in this place, the more I'm convinced the Fortress is more than capable of protecting itself, and is more concerned with my heart than my head." She smiled at him again, and he couldn't help but wonder if she was right. If only she knew what he had been through. But then, perhaps he didn't want her to. He'd given her enough loss without grieving her more. Instead, he asked her to dance.

"Of course," she smiled up at him with that sweet innocence that sent his heart pounding in his ears. Slowly, they shuffled out to the dance floor. Though they'd been going through the motions for months, Ever felt something different tonight as he took Isa's crooked hand in one of his own and her waist in the other. A voice inside him raged as he realized the hand that held hers looked just as thin and frail beneath the glove. Likewise, the hunch in his back put them eye to eye. Her good hand held his left arm, and if it hadn't been for all his clothes, could have nearly encircled it.

The familiar shame filled him as he recalled how far he'd fallen. Just a year ago, his arm had been solid and four times as large as it was now. Isa was tall for a woman, but he would have still stood a good three inches above her. A year ago, he would have been able to protect this beautiful creature from anything that threatened to harm her. Now, she was probably just as capable of protecting herself, if not more.

He wondered if there was any possibility that she could ever see him not as a captor or a king, but as a man. Could she ever respect him? Could she look up to him, trust him to keep her safe? Could she desire him? Even as they danced, the warmth of her skin radiated through his gloves, and suddenly, the correct posture the dance commanded wasn't close enough. Somewhere in the back of his mind, Ever remembered his tutors' instructions about proper distances between a man and a woman, and it took all his willpower to adhere to them.

As the dance came to an end, however, he realized with panic that she was going to leave him, as she did every night. Sure enough, the music died. Instead of immediately turning back to her chambers, however, Isa seemed to suddenly be struggling as he was. Without thinking, he leaned forward slowly. Her breath was uneven as their faces touched. She lifted her chin just a little, and for a moment, his lips rested on hers.

Slowly, to his disappointment, Isa pulled away. Her eyes pierced his, full of fear. Bit by bit, her fingers loosed themselves from his own, and before he knew it, she had fallen back a step. Then two. Then, without a word, she was gone.

As Ever walked back to the Tower of Annals, guilt washed over him. Here he was, falling in love with her, and yet, as Garin had pointed out, he was pushing her toward a cliff from which there was no return. She clearly wasn't ready for him. But he was dying. He would have to continue with the plan.

Despite his determination to carry out his schemes, Ever was haunted that night by those midnight blue eyes. Large and frightened, they watched him as they had for all his life. And in his sleep, Ever couldn't help but weep.

CHAPTER 11

"You seem unhappy." Isa jumped a little as the prince sat down beside her on the stone bench. Usually she heard his approach by the shuffling of his feet, but she had been distracted this morning. Isa twirled the rose in her hands again, wondering how much Ever would really like to hear what was on her mind. Not that he'd been unkind to her as of late. In fact, he'd been more chivalrous than ever. In the week following their near kiss, however, she'd found herself avoiding him. She could see that it hurt him, but she really was at a loss for what to do.

The kiss had frightened her. It wasn't that she hadn't wanted him to kiss her. Every muscle in her body had wanted nothing more than to meet his lips on the balcony that night. But it frightened her that things could change so quickly. Ever had gone from being the evil prince who had ruined her life thrice to a sweet companion whose company she found herself craving more and more. What would her family say?

It was this sentiment that had brought her out here today. She couldn't bring herself to dance, but being outside made her feel a bit closer to home, now that the days were warmer and the sun shined more often. If she closed her eyes and focused, she could sometimes pretend she was back in her garden, sitting on the little stone wall behind the house.

She could almost hear her mother's tools scraping in the garden dirt, and Megane running around after the chickens. She wished so much that she could ask her mother for advice. Was this right? Were her feelings right? Isa imagined asking her mother, but she shied away from even imagining the responses of her father and Launce.

"Well," Ever's voice brought her back to the present. He'd dropped his eyes to the ground and begun to stand again. "I suppose if you–" But Isa grabbed his arm and pulled him back down.

"No, I'm sorry. I don't mean to be rude. I was just thinking about my family." She sighed as he settled in and looked at her expectantly. His eyes were serious, standing out from his haggard face even more than usual in the early spring sunlight that filtered through the clouds. She expected him to scoff or get angry, but instead, he simply nodded, so she continued. "I just wish I could tell them I'm safe. But even more than that," she paused shyly before finishing in a whisper, "that I'm happy." The prince stared at her for a moment before the apprehension melted off his face and he was suddenly left beaming. The expression looked a bit strange in the gaunt, ashen face, but it wasn't unpleasant either. Isa decided that she rather like it.

"I think that can be arranged. Is there a token, something you could send with a letter so that they would know it was from you? I'm afraid your father will trust little that I send." Isa laughed and nodded.

"I'll send this rose." Touching its petals, she added, "It's just about to bloom." Ever stood up again, still smiling.

"I'll send Garin since your father knows him. Perhaps he will believe the words of an old friend."

"Is he human again?" Isa sat on the edge of her seat suddenly, thrilled with the idea of seeing another familiar face. More servants were turning every day, but they were mostly the ones tending to her. Ever gave her an even bigger grin, suddenly looking a bit boyish.

"He gained his body back this morning, although I'm not entirely sure he was ever human to begin with." The joy in Ever's voice was infectious, and Isa found herself suddenly feeling lighthearted. Perhaps she would dance this morning after all.

Isa's good mood lasted throughout the remainder of the day and into the evening. Supper was more animated than usual as Ever kept her laughing with stories from when he was a small boy. Even dancing was less awkward. Ever didn't try to kiss her again, and Isa nearly allowed herself to enjoy the warmth of his arms.

When she laid down in bed that night, as the servants scurried around to prepare her bedchamber for the chill of the night, Isa imagined how her family would react to Garin's message. Her mother would cry, and Megane would snatch the rose up to dry and save it. Launce would let out a few insolent remarks to the Fortress steward, and Ansel, even more. But even with all the carrying on, Isa knew the rose would mean hope for them where there had been none before.

As the servants finished their tasks, and Isa began to drift off, she heard thunder in the distance. It grew closer as her eyelids grew heavier.

"Look at her." Startled, Isa's eyes flew open and she tried to sit up, searching in the darkness. Her fire was out and her room had grown cold, which was strange. The servants never let her fire go out.

"Cerise?" she called out nervously. But Cerise didn't answer. Instead, the strange woman spoke again into the night.

"Really, Captain, do you think this is necessary? After all, she doesn't know us. It seems a bit unfair." The stranger didn't sound sorry though.

"We never promised to play fair." This time, it was a man's voice, not as deep as Ever's, but menacing.

As he spoke, a large bird swooped down, narrowly missing Isa's head. As she tried to duck, she realized she was no longer lying in her bed, but was tied to a chair instead. Again, the beast dove at her, and this time, it hit her ear. Isa felt a sharp pain followed by a warm trickle that rolled down her neck. She thought she could make out something in the dark, two shadows, perhaps.

"Captain, you'll have her dead in five minutes if you keep this up. Let me handle this," the woman said impatiently. Without another word, the man disappeared, and only the woman's silhouette remained. She pulled up another chair and put it across from Isa, straddling it so she could rest her arms on its back. As her eyes adjusted, Isa could see that the woman was very handsome, but she immediately sensed that this woman was also was very, very dangerous.

Her slick black hair was pulled tightly back into a warrior's bun, and her dress was slit up both sides so that long legs wrapped in men's trousers could stick out. Her unladylike position on the chair and the muscles that ran up and down her bared arms made Isa feel even more nervous. Her green eyes were bright, and would have been beautiful if they hadn't been so threatening. Full lips curved into a strange smile as Isa finally met her gaze. It was only then that Isa realized the light that filled the room was coming from those eyes. They were filled with rings of golden flame.

"I'm sorry for the inconvenience," the woman gestured to Isa's bonds. "But I needed to talk with you, and I knew you would run before I had the chance to explain myself. The least you can do is listen to me, woman to woman. Then I'll be gone, I promise." Isa sat, petrified. Who was this terrifying creature, and where had they brought her? She tried to open her mouth to scream for Ever, Garin, the servants, anyone who would hear her, but nothing came out.

"See? This is why I had to tie you," the woman shook her head. "Since you obviously can't escape, and no one has heard you, you might as well listen to what I have to say." Isa thought out that for a moment before ceasing to struggle against her ropes. The woman had a point. Isa was going nowhere fast. She had no choice but to listen.

"I've been watching your dreams," the woman began. Isa wondered how that was even possible. "You were wise when you first arrived here, back when you hated him, feared him with everything in you." She gave Isa a coy smile and wagged her finger. "But just as all women are with him, you were drawn in. Oh yes," she chuckled at Isa's expression. "I've felt the draw, too. It was even stronger before he wasted away so. You should have seen him in his prime!" She pursed her lips then smiled for a moment before going on.

"But no matter what he says or does, you're going to always be his captive." Isa frowned, unsure of why this strange woman was telling her all this.

"He's changing," Isa squeaked, her voice nervous and her throat dry. "He's not the same person he used to be."

"He's stopped insulting you, so now you think he loves you?" All traces of a smile left the woman's face, and the gold fire of her eyes bored into Isa. "I was hoping you'd be wise enough to see through him as you did at first, but obviously you're not." Taking Isa's chin firmly in her hand, the woman jerked her face up so Isa had to look her in the eye. "He's using you, Isabelle. A man like that cannot love. For power he sold his soul and you along with it." Isa wanted to cover her ears and hide, but the woman continued to speak, and Isa continued to hear.

"You see, the prince wants to use your power for his own ends, to heal his own self. It doesn't have to be like that though. I'm offering now to let you help me. You'll be no one's captive, and your power will be sung of for generations to come! If you allow me, I can help you reach heights of glory you never dreamed of! Together, we could heal you, erase the scars this prince inflicted on you forever! There would be no limit to what we could do."

For a moment, her words painted a picture in Isa's mind. Freedom from the agonizingly slow gait, being recognized as more than just the cripple. What would it feel like, Isa wondered, to go wherever she wanted, to make her own destiny? A part of her yearned for that, for the freedom to go where she wanted and do as she wished. No rules, no restrictions, no one to tell her she was incapable.

It was then that Isa noticed the thin young man standing behind the woman. Ashen and glassy-eyed, he watched Isa numbly. Isa felt her mouth drop in horror at the sight of the familiar face.

"What's your decision?" The woman's voice snapped her attention back to their conversation.

"My decision?"

"You can join me!" The woman's eyes were bright and fierce as she leaned forward and put a hand on Isa's shoulder. "Together, we can take him down! You can have your revenge after all these years! You and I could rule this land together! Make it what we want!"

"I don't want revenge," Isa whispered. As soon as she uttered the words, the woman's eyes went flat, and the golden flames roared.

"Then you've made your choice." Roughly, she let go of Isa's jaw, and she and the sickly young man began to retreat into the darkness. Sweat began to drip down Isa's temples. When she blinked again, the woman was gone, but Isa's room was ablaze with the golden tongues of fire that had been dancing in the woman's eyes. Still tied to the chair, Isa screamed until her throat ached. The flames grew higher, and the smoke was making it harder to breathe by the second.

Gasping, Isa tried to stand so she could pull herself to the door, but all she succeeded in doing was tipping her chair over so her face was even closer to the blaze. She cried out in anguish as the flames began to lick her body. Spots began to fill her vision. Just as she was about to give up, however, a faint voice called her name.

She was too weak to respond. Agony filled her as she realized she would die alone in the inferno. And yet, the voice called again, slightly louder this time. And it didn't stop. Something cool touched her hand. Then her head. Slowly, she began to realize that the voice that called to her was actually singing. It was Ever's voice, and the words he used were in the ancient tongue he'd serenaded her with in the Tower of Annals. Little by little, the flames were quenched, and the cool of the night began to touch her burned, charred body. It seemed like years, but eventually, she was able to open her eyes.

To her surprise, she was still in her room. There was no fire, not even a single candle. Anxious faces surrounded her, however. Female servants were continually changing the cold clothes on her forehead. What surprised her most, however, was Ever. His eyes were closed and his face was strained. His whole body shook. He still sang, and as he sang, blue light encircled their clasped hands. Isa stared at it in wonder. She tried to find her voice, and only after a full minute of trying could she croak out his name.

"She's awake!" Gigi announced. The other servants surrounding her seemed to let out their breath at the same time. Finally, Ever opened his eyes and stopped singing. He continued to grip her hand, however.

"What happened?" she asked faintly. Ever took a deep, slow breath, as if it was difficult to even speak.

"It appears our enemy has noticed your growing strength. Unfortunately, with strength comes a greater sensitivity to the darkness she harnesses."

"I don't know what that means."

"It means you had a night terror. Nevina must have returned from gathering men."

"She spoke to me," Isa tried to swallow, suddenly remembering the woman's cruel words.

"Yes, she sometimes does that."

"Have you had one of these dreams before?" Ever nodded grimly.

"My sensitivity to the presence of the Tumenian power began when I was seven." Isa tried to imagine Ever with the type of night terror she'd just experienced, but that a child should suffer so was too horrible to dwell on. Ever finally let her hand go and leaned back in his chair. "Garin had to stay outside my door at night for a whole year while I learned to manage the dreams."

"Do you still have them?" Isa was nearly too afraid to ask.

"I do, but they no longer terrify me. They simply remind me of what I'm protecting my people from." In the moonlight, a strange look crossed Ever's face as he suddenly studied Isa with a critical eye. "What did she tell you?" The question caught Isa off guard. While the woman who had tried to kill her was anything but trustworthy, Isa suddenly wondered about her warning that Ever was using her. Could any of it be true?

"She told me lots of things," she said cautiously. "But it was more *whom* I saw that frightened me." Ever looked at her expectantly, so she continued. "There was a man behind the woman. He didn't speak, but he held her weapons as he stood behind her. He was deathly pale, and looked as though he might be starving." She sighed. "I knew him as a child. He was born with a bad lung. His parents fell into poverty as they searched far and wide for healing, but no herbalist or healer could help him. I haven't seen him since–I haven't seen him for years," she quickly amended, realizing she'd nearly told Ever of the Caregivers. While the prince had certainly changed since she'd arrived, she wasn't sure she wanted to tell him about how her young friend's parents had sent him off in hopes of a better life in Tumen. She doubted he would understand the desperation of the sick and their families that had led them to make such a decision. Ever was already shaking his head.

"He's a Chien."

"A Chien?" Ever nodded, a look of disgust on his face.

"It's the soldier's term for Destinian traitors. They are servants in the royal courts and on the battle lines, although the term *slaves* might be more accurate. Anyhow, they leave Destin thinking our northern neighbor, Nevina's father, will welcome them into the arms of grace for a long and happy life." Isa felt her heart falter for a moment. The young man had most definitely not looked happy or healthy.

"What do they do with them?" she asked unevenly.

"They cut their tongues out to ensure their silence and complete dependence. When they are thoroughly beaten in both body and spirit, they are given away to nobles and royalty, sometimes even influential commoners as free labor." Ever shook his head. "They often accompany their *benefactors* to royal gatherings." Under his breath he added, "Serves them right for leaving." At this, Isa's face grew hot as she blurted out,

"Well, thanks to you, I was nearly one of them!" Ever stared at her but said nothing, so Isa continued angrily. "Do you think those people leave because they want to? While your father was cutting off all supply to the churches for the sick and the lame, the Caregivers began telling people they could come with them, that they would hide them in their supply carts and bring them to a place where they would receive food and clothing. It was a new start, they promised, one that would allow the unfortunate to begin new lives, to find work and make a living for themselves."

"What stopped you?" The prince frowned unhappily.

Exhausted from the dream and the outburst, she leaned back into her pillows. "Our neighbors urged my father to send me for years. I might find a husband there, they argued, one who didn't mind a damaged wife. He outright refused until he met you." There was a long silence that stretched between them. The servants had slowed their frantic pace by now, but seeing her fatigue, Gigi gently laid another compress on her forehead.

"You musn't push yourself too hard," she murmured gently to Isa before giving Ever a very pointed look at the door. He missed it or ignored it, however, and spoke instead, a fierce look on his face.

"How did you know how to find these Caregivers?"

"They always wear black metal rings." At this, the fire in the prince's eyes leapt, and it was a moment before he spoke again.

"Another misstep." His voice was nearly inaudible.

"What?"

"My family," he said slowly, rubbing his eyes with both hands, "has long valued strength above all else. In earnest, we've sought to protect this kingdom as well as we can. But it seems in so emphasizing the strong, we've forgotten the weak. And now our enemies are in the heart of the kingdom being welcomed, even sheltered, thanks to our negligence." The sky was beginning to lighten as he stood up and turned to go. "Perhaps the Fortress is right to strip me of my power."

Isa could not sleep for a long time. The fear that the dreams would return mingled with what Ever had said. Whether the woman from her dreams agreed or not, Ever *was* changing. Isa still felt anxiety when she thought of the woman's words, but the touch of his hands, the way he'd trembled while he worked to bring her out of the dream was a comfort. No, the woman could not know everything as she pretended. As she considered these things, Gigi walked up and gently pushed Isa back into a sleeping position.

"You don't need to be afraid, my dear. Ever will guard your dreams until Garin gets back. My guess is that they chose tonight because Garin had to stay in town for the storm. It is easier for two men to be on guard than one." She looked about ready to move into the next room, but something in Isa's expression must have changed her mind. Instead, she sat on the edge of Isa's bed and drew her into a warm, soft embrace. Isa could have stayed in that hug forever. It was like feeling her mother's arms around her once again. She must have been more tired than she knew, however, for soon Gigi was gently laying her back into the pillows, where she drifted into directionless, unmemorable dreams.

CHAPTER 12

Ever couldn't remember a worse night since the curse had fallen. Drawing Isa from the dream had taken more power from him than he'd expected. And he'd nearly been too late.

After Garin had left with the message for Isa's family earlier that day, everything had gone on as usual. Supper had been enjoyable, and Isa had even seemed to enjoy dancing with him. When they'd finished, the air had smelled of rain. Ever looked forward to the sound of a thunderstorm lulling him to sleep. He'd hoped it would drench Nevina's men as they continued to wait at the foot of the mountain. They were untrained, and with Nevina still gone in search of more men, they might not know what to do in the face of such a storm.

The feeling of peace couldn't last, however. He'd felt it before the servants had run to him. The princess's return to the valley had jolted him from his own sleep. Her heavy, stifling aggression had wafted into his dreams just moments before Cerise, Isa's childhood friend, had come pounding on the tower door.

"Your Highness!" the servant woman had cried. "Gigi says you need to come to Isa's chambers!" Ever could hear the panic in the young woman's voice. "She says it's a night terror!" Ever had leapt off his pallet so quickly he'd nearly tripped and fallen on the floor. His sore bones and stiff muscles protested as he moved, but he hardly noticed them.

Staggering through the great halls as quickly as he could, he had begged the Fortress to protect her. He was angry with himself for not foreseeing this. Of course, the princess would choose to return from gathering more men for her army the night that Garin was gone. Soudain was a decently sized city, but word spread fast. Any spies Nevina had planted there would have reported quickly that Garin was in town, away from the Fortress. Garin had always made Nevina nervous, so she would have seen his absence as a golden opportunity. Nevina must have suspected that with only the prince guarding the Fortress's inhabitants, it would be easy to slip past him. And it had been. A cold, steely fear had gripped his heart as he imagined all of the horrible things the princess could be doing to Isa.

When he'd arrived, the young woman had been unresponsive to his initial attempts to draw her from the nightmare. He'd cursed the princess as he struggled to keep Isa from falling completely into her grasp. Her face was ghostly, and sweat sheened her skin. As her breathing faltered, Ever had desperately poured even more strength into drawing the poison from her mind. For a moment, it felt as if he was losing his father again. But no, a part of his mind had whispered to him. This would be worse.

Hours had passed as he'd gripped her soft, crooked hand in his own bent claws. The servants had watched in panic. Nothing like this had happened in the Fortress since he was a small child, and few of them had ever been privy to those awful episodes, spare Garin, Gigi, and the few servants who had assisted them. Not even his parents had known about the horrible nights he'd passed, screaming as the darkness had tried time and time again to poison his mind. And this time they were doing it to Isa.

Now that it was all over, Ever was more exhausted than he'd ever been in his life, and yet, he couldn't sleep. The new knowledge that Nevina was handing out weapons of her power to these strange Caregivers in Soudain disturbed him. How long had the Tumenians been infiltrating the capitol, and wearing weapons of dark magic at that? King Rodrigue had once suggested they create similar weapons for their own men, talismans that held a bit of the monarchs' strength. Ever had pleaded with him not to, however. Such power wasn't meant for just anyone, only those the Fortress had chosen, he insisted. Ever had been grateful when his father listened to him, but apparently, the idea was not original to his father. Who knew how many men Nevina now had in Soudain, armed with her twisted rings?

He hobbled over to the great wardrobe in the center of the room. A weak shine spilled out from the wardrobe as he removed the ring from its case. Sitting, he turned it over again and again in his hands.

If he'd removed this ring ten years ago, it would have lit the whole tower in its brilliance the moment he'd touched it. Even a year ago, the ring had still shined for him when they'd taken it from the queen's finger and given it to him for safekeeping. Now its shine was little more than a reflection from the sun that was just beginning to rise. As he held the ring, shame warred with desperation as it never had before.

Ever fell into a restless sleep with the ring in his hand. When he awakened, it was nearly noon, and he could see Isa venturing out to the rose garden. He had a sudden urge to go to her. Without thinking, he put the ring away and made his way down to the girl. She was already dancing by the time he arrived. He stood at the edge of the walk so as not to startle her. When she finally stopped, he could see her cheeks were flushed with the effort and there were dark circles beneath her eyes. She wore an expression of deep concentration as she danced today. When she heard him approach, however, she stopped and dipped into a quick curtsy.

"Do you mind if I watch?" Ever gestured to the stone bench nearby. She gave him a wry smile.

"My guess is that you've *been* watching, otherwise you wouldn't have known where to find me." Ever smiled and conceded it was thus. He was impressed as she resumed her movements. Compared to the first time he'd seen her, her legs had grown noticeably stronger, and she was more confident. A tranquil smile lit her face as she moved, and sometimes, she closed her eyes briefly as she slowed to make a movement just right.

"Where did you learn?" he asked when she was finished. A bit breathless, Isa sat down beside him.

"I started dancing when I was very small, really too young. I would go watch the Soudain dancers practice when I was four, and I would mimic them. Madame Nicolette saw me and decided that I had some talent."

"I remember her," Ever said. "She brought her students to the Fortress to perform at celebrations. I remember hearing they performed at official city events as well." Isa nodded.

"She took me under her wing, and I became her special pupil as I grew older." Isa's eyes got a far-off look. "I'm not sure if I was really as good as she claimed, or if it was simply all the extra instruction, but by the time I was eight, there was talk that I would–" She stopped suddenly and shook her head at the ground. "It doesn't matter now. That was a long time ago." The wistfulness in her voice made Ever suddenly uncomfortable. Still, for some morbid reason, he wanted to know.

"Please tell me." After a moment of thought, Isa spoke slowly.

"There was talk that I would be her lead dancer by the time I was twelve." Ever sat quietly as the entire weight of his foolish boyhood actions crashed down over him. In addition to all the other things he had taken from her, this future had been stolen as well. As always, there was one more sin, one more piece of her life that he had stolen in his youthful foolishness and never sought to repair.

"I'm sorry," was all he could say. He didn't dare to look into her eyes.

"I think that's the reason I was so angry for so many years." When she spoke, however, Isa's voice wasn't tearful as he feared it would be, but thoughtful instead. "I felt like I'd been robbed of my purpose, like I had no other reason to survive other than *not* to be a burden to my family. I needed to be needed."

"You're needed here," Ever gently cupped her face and turned it so that she had to look into his eyes. As he touched her, he couldn't help but notice the strange ripples of energy that it sent through him. She gazed back at him and to his delight, she didn't pull away.

"Why?" She breathed. "Why do you need *me*?"

"I'm not sure why the Fortress chose you," he admitted, still touching her face. "But the Fortress doesn't choose people by accident. What I do know is that we needed a light in the darkness of the curse, a beacon to follow in the night. *You* have been and will continue to be that light." He let go of her chin, but ran his fingers lightly across her jawbone, and to his surprise, she smiled hesitantly. Gingerly, he pulled his hand back before it decided to touch her again on its own accord. "Do you feel like you're needed now?" She studied him for what felt like a long time before answering,

"I'm beginning to." An idea hit him, and with it, a pang of guilt, but he acted upon it anyway.

"Come with me. I need to show you something." Back in the Tower of Annals, he went to the wardrobe for the second time that day and opened up the case. "This is the Queen's Ring. Every queen has worn this since the Fortress was created."

"It's lovely," Isa whispered, staring wide-eyed at the silver ring. A large, round blue crystal was surrounded by smaller white crystals that lay in silver vines weaving in and out of one another. Still holding the ring, Ever took her over to the full-length oval mirror that stood near one of the window walls. Gently, he pressed the ring into her right palm.

"Now," he pointed to mirror. "Look." Isa gasped as she gazed into the glass. Her eyes flamed bright blue, and the ring threw bright streaks of its own light across the room as she held it.

"What's happening?" she murmured.

"It's been there since you arrived. You just weren't ready to see it yet. Until now." Taking her by the shoulders, he pulled her away from the mirror to face him. "You are stronger than you think, Isabelle."

"But . . . I don't know what to do with it, or even how it works!" she protested, looking back into the mirror.

"I can teach you!" he insisted, hoping to quell her fears before she thought too long about them. "And the Fortress will give you what you need! Your power is still young, and yet you can't deny that you've brought the Fortress back to life!" Isa frowned a bit.

"You're still not healed. And neither are the soldiers." Ever wished briefly he hadn't told her about the stone army that stood on the back lawn.

"You will be capable of even more very soon. Trust me." The words tasted as he spoke them. As he took the ring back, it immediately dulled at his touch. She eyed him suspiciously, but he gently took her hand and led her to the door. "I will see you tonight. We will have much to discuss, but you need to rest first. Last night was a long one." She gave him a funny look, but finally nodded before heading down the steps. As she left, Garin walked up.

"Sire," he gave Ever a long look up and down with a dissatisfied expression. "You should be resting."

"I take it you've heard."

"The servants can speak of nothing else," Garin frowned as he poured a glass of nectar tea and handed it to the prince. "I thought Nevina might try something while I was gone, but I didn't think she would be so bold. However, I see the night's events haven't frightened Isabelle off completely."

"She's ready, Garin," Ever was turning the small ring over in his hands once more. Garin frowned again, even more deeply, the thin lines on his forehead wrinkling in disapproval.

"If that's so, then why do you look so guilty?" When Ever didn't answer, his expression softened a bit. "You love her, don't you?" Ever still couldn't answer. His mentor, however, was too familiar with his ways to be fooled. "You know you could heal her now."

"I would if I could!" Ever threw his hands up in frustration. "But I don't have much strength left! Garin, you know as well as I do that if my flame is extinguished I'll die." he shook his head and walked over to the window wall to stare at the great valley below him. "I'll pay her back one day. I'll make it right. One day, she'll understand . . . ." His voice trailed off. He wasn't even convincing himself, let alone the steward.

"Or," Garin interjected, "She'll be unprepared and vulnerable, and she won't be able to heal you. You will die, and she'll be left to rule a cursed castle without a guide or companion." He shook his head. "What kind of life is that for the woman you love?"

"What choice do I have?" Ever exploded. He dropped into a chair and buried his head in his hands. "Either way I die. Either way, I lose her." Garin's voice was kinder this time as he softly called the prince by the nickname he'd given him as a small boy.

"Ever, has it crossed your mind that perhaps the Fortress hasn't done all of this simply to spite you? That perhaps there is a lesson to be learned?" Ever looked at him miserably, so he continued. "If she was truly ready, she wouldn't have trembled so as she ran down those steps just now. Gigi says we nearly lost her last night. Just as you weren't ready when you were seven, I'm telling you, she's not ready now. Trust the Fortress! You weren't born with your strength by accident, and she wasn't brought here by chance. There's a purpose in all of this, I promise! The Fortress never forsakes its chosen! The fact that it brought

Isa to you should be proof enough for that." But Ever shook his head.

"Unfortunately, I've seen too much to hold onto such a childish hope as that, as much as I would like to." And with that, he slipped the ring into his pocket. After last night's assault, it was clear the Fortress no longer cared what befell them inside its own walls. He would have to do this on his own.

CHAPTER 13

As soon as she returned to her chambers, Gigi fussed at Isa until she agreed to lie down and sleep before dinner. It was hard to sleep, however. The memory of last night's terror still lingered fresh in her mind. Even stronger than the memory of the terror though, was the strange excitement she felt in her body and soul as she tried to close her eyes.

It was strange to think that just at the end of last summer, she'd been abandoned and directionless. Now, at the dawn of this spring, she had both a purpose and, she hoped, someone who cared as much about her as much as she did him. The way he'd looked at her that morning sent shivers up her spine, the way he'd protected her last night through her terrors, the way he believed in her when she couldn't believe in herself were all pieces of a dream she couldn't have imagined last year. And when he'd touched her face, it had awakened a strange desire within her, filling her with a kind of longing she hadn't felt for anyone before, not even Raoul. For Gigi's sake, she pretended to sleep, but really, all Isa could do was think of Ever.

Her act of sleeping must have looked real enough because the servants began to speak to one another in the next room over. Not quite ready to get up yet, she laid there quietly, and Isa soon found herself drawn into their discussion. She knew it was rude to eavesdrop, but the conversation was taking a turn she couldn't ignore.

"Do you think it's true? That the prince will propose tonight?" The younger servant's voice was full of excitement and intrigue.

"Gigi says we must not talk about such things. It's not our place." Cerise's voice was less enthusiastic. She lowered it to add, "I'll admit though, I'm worried. I don't think she's ready. I just wish he would give her more time."

"But he doesn't have time!" the younger one argued. "His fire burns duller with each day! At least, that's what Solomon says."

"Then I'm afraid he might be too late." Cerise sighed. "Perhaps Prince Everard was never meant to be king. Perhaps he was meant to prepare the way for her. At least if we must lose him, we would have someone to follow in his place." There was sadness in Cerise's voice. She spoke so softly now that Isa had to strain to hear, the deafening beat of her heart making it nearly impossible to listen in.

"But the curse demands that she heal him, or the rest of it will never be fulfilled!" Isa's mouth fell open in horror. The curse demanded? Panic filled her. How was she supposed to heal Ever, especially if he was as close to death now as they made it sound? The younger servant spoke again, this time in a comforting voice.

"Perhaps she is ready. Every time she's on the crystal floor it shines more brightly. And she's brought back most of the Fortress! She brought us back!"

"I think we should be done talking of such things now," Cerise's voice was cross. "And I think that no matter what we say or do or think, he will be proposing soon. That was his plan from the start, so we'd better be ready."

Isa lay in a miserable daze. She wished this was a nightmare Ever or Garin could pull her from. She'd known at the beginning of her stay at the Fortress that Ever's designs were self-serving. How could they not be? He'd blackmailed Ansel with the lives of his family to get Isa to the Fortress. Then, when she'd arrived, he'd given her such looks of cold disdain and hatred that she wondered why he'd summoned her in the first place.

But then Ever had begun to change. Isa was sure he had. The gentle words he spoke to her, the way he looked at her, the confidence he'd had in her, the trembling in his fingers every time he reached for her hand or her face. He certainly wasn't the same man she'd met last fall. Or perhaps, just perhaps, he was a very good actor. The woman's words came back to her from the night before.

For power he sold his soul and you along with it.

He'd lied by failing to tell her of the curse's requirement that she heal him, and he'd failed to mention his approaching death. He was apparently pushing her towards an end the servants didn't think she was ready for, whatever it was.

Soon after that, Gigi and her hoard of handmaidens arrived to prepare Isa for supper as they always did. Isa allowed them to dress her in whatever they wanted in whatever way they wished to do it. For weeks now, the bathwater had been clean, and the clothes had been fresh. Tonight, however, they were more than meticulous as they readied her. Gigi ran around, shaking her head at everything they did, clucking her tongue and demanding they do it again. She, too, seemed on edge.

That night's gown was more exquisite than any Isa had ever laid eyes on. It was a deep blue crushed velvet.

Ribbons wove through the waist with pearls and diamonds, and the arms were draped with gold lace. The blue parted at the bottom to reveal skirts of cream colored silk. Without a word Isa allowed them to pull it over her head and fuss with it to their hearts' desires. Once, she caught Gigi's eye. As they looked at one another, she nearly began to cry. Gently, Gigi laid a soft hand on her cheek and gave her a sad smile.

"You look like a princess, my dear." Isa wanted to weep. Instead, she stepped into her boots and let them finish fixing her hair. Finally, she heard the dreaded knock at the door. It was time.

When the door opened, Isa's heart flopped in her chest. He was holding a single rose, looking as nervous as she felt. Instead of his black hood, he wore a deep blue coat and fitted black trousers, and his boots were polished so that they reflected the light of the fire in her hearth. He trembled a bit as he stood there, and his face looked thinner than ever. His hunch was so deep now that she stood a bit taller than he. And yet, she wanted him so badly it made her heart ache. The fire in his eyes flamed brighter for a moment when he saw her. Finally, he cleared his throat.

"My lady, would you join me?" Nodding, she accepted his arm. Neither of them spoke as they slowly made their way to the dining hall. Isa was sure he could hear her heart trying to beat out of her chest, and she didn't dare meet his eyes until he walked them right through the dining hall and out onto the balcony. Sitting her down on one of the dozens of stone benches that surrounded the crystalline floor, he sat beside her and took her hands in his gloved ones.

"I can honestly say I never thought it would be this way," he finally said. Isa looked up at him but said nothing. "When you arrived, I thought I was getting one more person to help solve the puzzle. I never expected you to change so many things." He swallowed hard before continuing. "For years, the memory of you tormented me, and I hated you even more when you showed up. But there was nothing I could do. You were here, and I had to use any means I could to break the curse.

"But you," he was suddenly staring into her eyes with that strange, disarming look of his. "You began to teach me that there is healing in love. I think I began to love you without even being aware of it. The night you ran out though . . . ," he shook his head and his jaw clenched a bit at the memory. "I thought I'd lost you. I hadn't realized how much I needed you." He took a deep breath.

"That fool from Soudain didn't deserve you, and I'm glad he ran like a coward. You are too rare a creature to belong to someone like him." Isa's heart cracked a little more with each word he spoke. She wanted so desperately to believe him, but with each confession of love, he failed to confess his secrets. He was still lying to her even now as he moved stiffly from the bench to drop down on one knee.

"I love you, Isabelle Marchand. Will you marry me?" Isa's heart plunged and soared as he spoke the words. Her conflicting desires raged inside of her as she stared at the ring he pulled from his pocket. She wanted to desperately to say yes. She loved him deeply. In a way, her heart already was and would always be his. And yet, angry tears threatened to fall as she knew he still hadn't told her the truth. Cerise's words echoed in her mind as she gazed miserably at his expression of hope. He would die if she couldn't heal him soon. She couldn't let him die. Without a word, she stretched out her hand. Perhaps she could make herself ready. She had to. Her hand shook as he slipped it into the Queen's Ring.

As she did so, the air around them began to quiver. A column of blue fire shot up into the air to the heavens, engulfing them. Isa screamed as she saw the true power of the Fortress for the first time. She felt the weight of new burdens settling on her shoulders. Destin's well-being and the faces of its citizens began to flash before her. A familiar heat beat at her back, and she recognized the heat of the evil fire that had nearly consumed her the night before.

Isa struggled to stay upright as the burdens and enemies began to settle upon her. She tried to steel herself, to face the evil that challenged the light. She tried to memorize the people's faces. She clenched her jaw and looked at the young man before her. Reaching out with trembling fingers, she tried to touch him, to heal his wounds. Before she could reach him, however, she felt her strength give way. It all began to collapse around her. The evil advanced, and the cry of innocent blood echoed in her ears as she failed to hold it all up. Yanking the ring off, she shoved it at Ever, and the column immediately disappeared. The only sound left was her haggard choking. The servants had been right. The woman from her dream had been right. He had been using her.

"I'm not ready!" she sobbed. She could nearly hear the sound of her heart tearing in half. She had wanted so much to be ready. Her soul had longed to find his words of confidence in her fulfilled. Why couldn't it all be true? Anger began to mix with the heartache as she gasped, trying to catch her breath. He had known she wasn't ready. And he'd still asked.

She felt Ever try to place his hand on her shoulder, but Isa shoved it off. "How could you do that to me?" She choked out as tears ran down her face. "I trusted you!" The prince hesitated, looking torn. "Tell me about the curse!" she demanded. "Tell me all that you hid from me!" After another moment of hesitation, he closed his eyes and finally began to recite.

"*Before life can be found in this sacred place once again, a new strength must be found. What has been broken must be remade. The one who was strong must be willing to die. Only then can the Fortress and the kingdom again have the protector they deserve.*" After he finished speaking, he reached again for her, but she drew back.

"So I was supposed to heal you? How can the broken heal the broken? I thought you loved me, Everard, but I can see now that all along I was just part of your plan!" Anger pulsed through her as she waited for an answer. Ever stared at her with a long, sorrowful look. Suddenly, he tilted his head and closed his eyes as if he was listening to something. It was a moment before he spoke, and when he did, his voice was cold.

"If that's how you feel, then there is no place for you here." Stiffly, he drew himself to his feet. His face lost all of its openness, and suddenly, he looked like a soldier. "Garin," he called. The steward ran over, his own face deeply sorrowful. "Put Isabelle in one of the carriages. You are to take her as far from Destin as you can. She is never to return." Isa felt a wave of horror wash over her.

"Wait!" she cried out. "What are you doing? I turn down your proposal, and you send me into *exile*?" But no matter how many demands she made or how much she begged, he wouldn't consent. He wouldn't even discuss it. Despite her protests, Garin gently took her by the shoulders and led her from the balcony, leaving Ever alone to stare stonily down at the statues.

Gigi was instructed to get her into proper riding gear. The mood was one of tension and fear as the servants scurried about her room. Her gown was exchanged for a soft leather riding skirt and a simple white shirt under her mother's cloak. Isa tried in vain to ask Gigi and Cerise what was going on, but no one would tell her. Before she left, however, Gigi drew her into a tight embrace before handing her the bag she'd first brought to the Fortress. By the weight of it, Isa could tell its contents had been added to.

Without time for proper goodbyes, she was whisked away to the stables where a coach, all black, awaited her. Isa tried one more time to beg Garin to allow her to speak with Ever, but he gently shook his head and drew her inside. Isa left the Fortress more confused and hurt than she'd been when she'd arrived.

"Why?" She turned miserably to Garin, who sat on the padded bench across from her. "Why would he do all of this, push me too fast and then send me away? I want to help! I just don't know how."

"I know you do, my dear," Garin said kindly. "But you are not ready, and that's why you couldn't accept the Queen's Ring. The prince does not want you near when the Tumenian princess attacks." Isa felt the blood drain from her face.

"They're going to attack? But the army! It's not ready! And Ever's so weak!" Garin nodded gravely.

"We don't know when, but the prince senses it will be soon."

"But why do I have to go so far? That means it will take a long time for you to return!"

"Princess Nevina won't be satisfied with simply taking the prince's life. She knows who you are now, and she knows that you are valuable to him. If she found you, and she will try, she would commit acts of unfathomable cruelty against you out of spite. So no, I won't be returning." Isa stared at him in shock. From the prince's birth on, and even while bound to a shadow's existence, Garin had rarely left Ever's side. And now he was leaving his charge forever in order to protect her.

Even more surprising was Ever's last act of chivalry. He'd prepared himself for certain death by sending his most trusted confidante away to keep Isa safe. But she couldn't leave, Isa realized suddenly. Not yet. As deeply as he'd wounded her, she couldn't just let him die. Desperately, she tried to think of something, anything that might change the steward's mind, or at least delay her departure.

"Please, just . . . just let me see my family one more time before I go. I need to let them know that I'm safe, and that I'm free." Garin glared at her, but didn't immediately refuse her request. "One day." She reached out and took his leathery hand. "I just need one night and one day with them." Finally, Garin nodded his head. Isa nearly collapsed with relief, but leaned back against the coach instead. She'd bought herself one chance to escape.

It was late by the time the coach reached her family's stables. Launce was the first one to see her. He shouted for the others as he sprinted toward them. Within seconds, everyone was there, hugging her, laughing, and crying. It took Isa a while to untangle herself so she could point out Garin's presence. Ansel's greeting wasn't nearly as enthusiastic as it had once been, but he did at least invite the steward inside.

"My Isa!" Deline held her tightly and whispered her name over and over again as if she were a small child. Isa wished she could stay in her mother's arms forever and never let go. But all too soon, they followed everyone else inside. Isa's heart was heavy as she thought about the heartbreak that was about to take place.

"I assume you're home to stay?" Ansel posed it as a question, but with the threatening look he shot at Garin, Isa knew he wasn't giving her a choice. Garin was about to answer, but she spoke quickly, sending him a warning look.

"I wanted to see you," she simply said. Isa knew she was just putting off the inevitable, but perhaps they could have one night of joy before she had to hurt them again. Launce, Megane, and Ansel began to pepper her with questions, but much to Isa's relief, Deline saw how tired she was. It wasn't long before she was tucked in her little bed with Megane snuggling at her side.

Isa thought back to how miserable she'd been the last time she'd slept in the cozy attic room. Now, she would give anything just to have more time there with her little sister by her side and her parents and brother downstairs. Garin had chosen to sleep in the stable with the coachman, so Deline, always the gracious host, had made sure they had more blankets than they could possibly use. This annoyed Isa, as it meant she couldn't sneak out at night, but escape would simply have to wait until the morning. As much as she needed to stay awake and plan her flight, sleep's call was too strong, and she soon succumbed.

The next morning, she woke up later than she'd wanted to. The sun was already high, and judging from the smells wafting up from the kitchen, everyone else had already eaten. Isa threw a brush through her hair and headed downstairs quickly. As she ate her biscuits and fruit, Deline told her that Garin had gone into the town to look at some official council reports with Ansel. The morning passed quietly and quickly as Isa soaked up every detail, every smell and sound of her old home. But she found no peace. As much as she wanted to stay there forever, another calling tugged at her heart. And she knew this time she couldn't ignore it.

She excused herself that afternoon to go walking around town. She took Megane to keep from rousing suspicion with her family. It was cool enough that Isa was able to bring her cloak along and draw the hood. Despite her limp, few people recognized her in the bustle of the busy day, which gave her time to think. How could she change Garin's mind? Changing his mind would be easier than trying to escape on her own. But Garin was Ever's most loyal servant and companion, the least likely to disobey him. That also meant, however, that he would also want to spare Ever's life. Isa would have to use that to her advantage.

Isa and Megane reached the market quickly. Isa couldn't help but notice how little was for sale. Just last spring, every stall had been filled with ripe, brightly colored fruits and vegetables, fresh bread, salted fish, wild game, and even sweets and pastries. Just as the food in the Fortress had been sparse and bland when she'd arrived, so it was here, but even more so. The sickness of the Fortress seemed to have seeped out of its borders and into the kingdom. Fear made Isa shiver as she realized just how much was at stake under the weight of the curse. It went far beyond Ever and his soldiers, or even the walls of the Fortress. Isa suddenly felt a pang of sympathy for the prince. She was beginning to understand why he was so very desperate.

As Isa walked the streets of her town, she also realized it wasn't enough. Even the time with her family, as precious as it had been, wasn't enough anymore. She'd gotten everything she'd wanted and prayed for. She was home and her family was safe, and yet, she felt emptier than she'd ever felt in her life. Somehow, the man who had made her life so miserable had become its shining star. As this revelation came to her, Isa was pulled back into her surroundings by a cry of delight from Megane.

"Isa! Look! The Caregivers are back! So many of them!" Looking up, Isa saw dozens of the coaches filling the marketplace. She had to work to keep the horror from her face as Megane ran off in search of Marko, and it took everything in Isa not to call after her. That would raise suspicion.

"Isabelle? Isabelle Marchand?" A familiar voice called out to her, despite her cloak. Turning, she saw her old neighbor hurrying toward her.

"Hello, Margot," she forced herself to smile.

"You're back!" The plump woman stopped and gaped at her. She didn't gape long enough, however, to let Isa speak. "You're just in time! They'll be leaving tonight!" Isa frowned.

"Who's leaving?"

"Why, the Caregivers! Marko says they're putting an end to the prince's abuse! Tonight, they're going to take us, anyone who wants, right from under his nose!" A chill ran down Isa's spine. Just the memory of the flaming arrows and diving hawks made her leg tingle.

"You're sure it's tonight?" Isa struggled to keep her voice under control. Margot nodded joyfully.

"Just think, dear! You and your family will finally be free of that wretched monster locked away in the Fortress!" Whirling around, Isa began to call for Megane, but just as she spotted her sister, another familiar face appeared.

"Isa!" Marko boomed, holding his arms out. Terror gripped Isa as she grabbed Megane's hand. Pushing her body as fast as it would go, she took off in the other direction. Her ankle kept her from going far, however, so Isa turned down the first alley she could find, away from the crowds and mostly hidden from sight.

"Megane," she whispered breathlessly. "I need you to do something for me. It's of the utmost importance. It will keep you and Launce and Mother and Father safe. But you must do exactly as I say. Can you do that?"

"What about you? You just came home!" Megane whimpered. Leaning down, Isa kissed the girl's face and drew her into a tight hug.

"I know, Megs," she said. "But if I don't do this, many people will get hurt. I'm counting on you. Now, can you help me?" Wiping away tears, Megane nodded. "Alright, I need you to go home and tell Mother and Father that I love them very much. Tell them that I'm going away to keep them safe." Before she could send her little sister off, however, a man's large frame loomed at the entrance of the alley. Marko watched them, his face dark.

"I wish you wouldn't have done that," he said as he began to walk toward them. Isa pushed Megane behind her as she stood to face the Caregiver. For the first time, she noticed his black metal ring glowing a dull gold as he tightened his right hand into a fist.

"Run, Megane!" Isa screamed, shoving the little girl as far behind her as she could. Marko reached out and grabbed Isa roughly.

"I didn't want to do this, believe me," he said as he pinned her against the wall. She tried to scream, but he covered her face with his hand. "But you just *had* to take his side. And my princess can't forgive that." Isa struggled, but he was too strong. She began to see spots as he kept his hand clamped over her mouth and nose. "You don't have to worry about him suffering for too long," he whispered in her ear. "He won't last much longer with or without you." Without thinking, Isa cried out to the Fortress for help, that ever present companion she'd come to count on. She wasn't sure why, but it was all she could think to do.

At that moment, something sparked inside of her. It felt familiar, and yet, she'd never felt it like this before. It came from her heart and flowed through the rest of her body. As it moved down her arms, Marko gave a cry of pain and flew backward, smacking his head against the building behind them. Blue liquid flame shot out of Isa's fingertips, nearly blinding her as it flared all around. The force of it nearly made her lose her own balance. Relief at being safe from Marko was followed by panic as Isa realized she couldn't move. The blue flame had engulfed her completely, and she stood frozen with her arms stretched out at her sides as it continued to flow out of her and into the man on the ground.

"Isabelle!" Garin's voice sounded from a distance. Isa wanted so much to cry out, to scream for help, but she couldn't move. Just seconds later, though, cool, rough hands had taken her own, and the flame was channeling into them. They stood that way for what felt like an eternity. In amazement, she watched as Garin took the brunt of the raw power that streamed from her. He looked back into her eyes, and suddenly, the older man who had bowed to Ever's every wish no longer looked like a castle steward. Instead, he looked like something completely other, something powerful. His eyes blazed a bright blue, and his skin became white like snow. The lines of age that edged his eyes and mouth disappeared. His arms were powerful, and just for a second, Isa thought she glimpsed a pair of large silver wings on his back. Whether vision or truth, however, it only lasted for the blink of an eye. Slowly, the flame began to ebb, and bit by bit, Isa could move again. As it slowed, Garin began to look more like himself again.

"What was that?" Isa gasped.

"That was the strength."

"No, what you just did! How did you do that?" Isa searched his face for answers, but instead of giving them to her, Garin gave her a small smile.

"You don't think the Maker would forge such a great source of power as the Fortress without giving it a steward, do you?"

"That was amazing though," Isa could only bring herself to whisper. "Garin, what are you?"

"Just a simple servant, my dear."

"But–"

"There is no one servant more important than another. My purpose is simply a bit . . . different than that of the others. But we don't have time for this kind of talk. We need to be off in the morning." Before he was finished speaking, however, Isa was already heading back toward the street, thankful that Megane had escaped. They walked as quickly as they could back toward Isa's home. Instead using the front door, however, Isa went directly to the stable.

"And where do you think you're going?" Garin demanded to know as Isa led her father's horse from his stall.

"I'm going back. The princess is attacking tonight."

"And how do you know this?" Isa gave an impatient huff as she began to saddle the horse. They didn't have time for this.

"The Caregivers have arrived in town, more than I've ever seen before. I was told they're planning to take the kingdom by force. They're clearing the streets first, however, by offering to *save* those of us who want to escape it. Nevina must have won them over to her side as well."

"And you think I should just let you waltz off into the arms of the enemy?" Isa stopped and looked straight at him.

"We can help Ever."

"Absolutely not!" Garin fired back. "You're coming with me. Now. We're leaving this place, just as Everard instructed! If something happened to you, your blood would be on my head! Do you remember a word I said about what they will do to you?"

"It doesn't matter," Isa shook her head and climbed up onto the horse. "He needs me." As she spoke, thin blue flames licked the reigns, making the horse whinny loudly. "I'm going, Garin, and you're welcome to come with me if you desire."

"And what makes you so sure you can help him after what happened last night?"

"Last night, I didn't understand. I couldn't see that because the Fortress has chosen me, it will give me the strength that I need to bear the burden." She hoped he wouldn't see how her hands were trembling as she waited for his answer. Garin stood with his arms folded, watching her with an unreadable expression. Finally, a smile slowly spread across his face.

"Alright," he bowed his head in concession.

"You mean you're coming with me?"

"I mean you're ready."

CHAPTER 14

"Please!" Ever's shout echoed down the stairs as he slammed his fist on the stone wall of the tower. "Come back to me! I'm doing all I can!" Instead of answering, however, Fortress stayed silent, and Ever felt his heartbeat fall out of rhythm, just enough to bring him to his knees. As he knelt to try and catch his breath, he went over the night before for the thousandth time in his head. What had gone wrong?

If Garin had been there, he would have said that Ever needed to just trust the Fortress. But really, Ever wondered, what could possess him to trust the very force that had stolen the life from his body and left him alone and cursed? He'd hoped that Isa could be made ready by a speedy marriage. The ring would focus her strength, he'd assured himself. It would make up for whatever she was still lacking. But it hadn't, and at the moment when he could have tried to pick up the pieces, his straying senses had picked up the sound of damnation. Nevina's battle horn had sounded.

It had taken all of his willpower to harden his face as he exiled the girl he loved. Not that it would help in the end. His enemy was brutal and cruel, and he knew it was only a matter of time before she turned her rage on Isa when he was dead and gone. Nevina would hunt her down. Sending Garin with her was the only way he could think of to send her with any shred of hope.

As they'd prepared her to leave, a small voice in his head had whispered that he could heal her as a parting gift.

But no, he'd thought. That would have taken all of his remaining strength, and without it, he would die. *You'll die anyway*, his conscious had prodded. *If I'm dead*, he'd snapped at the annoying voice, *who will be here to guard the kingdom one last time*? And so he'd sent her away to her doom. The look on her face was heartbreaking, the same expression she'd worn as a small child when he'd broken her the first time. Only this time, breaking her had felt like losing a piece of himself. Never had he felt so vulnerable. She hadn't seen it, but tears had run down his face as he'd watched her coach race off into the night. And now, there was nothing left for him to do but beg and plead with a Fortress that had long since abandoned the prince it had once loved.

"I don't understand!" He shouted up at the soaring arches. "Isa had a new strength!" *But she didn't stay*, the voice of reason whispered in his head. "She brought healing!" he argued. *But she didn't heal everything*. "What about me?" he pleaded desperately. "I was strong, and I've been willing to die. My whole life I've been willing to die! How many times have I gone into battle and risked my life?" *You don't seem ready to die now*.

No matter how much he begged, the Fortress remained cold and silent. There was no comforting presence, no gentle peace that he'd once taken for granted. Beaten, he stood painfully and went back to the window wall to look at the army's progress below.

They would be at the gates within minutes. The halls were silent beneath him, as he'd given the servants instructions to hide as best as they could. The hope he'd given them was vain. He hadn't told his loyal friends how their enemies would silence them forever, how they would break their bodies and their spirits. It was easier to force a smile and tell Gigi that she and the others might make it if they stayed quiet for long enough. But deep down, he knew that even if he'd retained his strength, he could not fight an entire army on his own. His men were still statues on the field.

Anger boiled within him as he thought about how the Fortress was no longer even protecting those within its walls. He could feel the emptiness in the air. The presence that had once guided and guarded him seemed content now to watch from afar as they all burned.

He drew his sword from his sheath, as he'd done so many times, but this time, he did so knowing it was pointless. He could see it now, how he'd strayed, how he'd forgotten the straight path that he'd run so confidently as a child. It was too late to fix that, but perhaps, his broken heart hoped, at least he could leave this world with some honor. The Fortress wouldn't strip him of that as well, would it?

He stood with the sword at his side as the Chiens did as they were instructed. He could smell the smoke as they began to set his beloved world ablaze. He could imagine the intricate tapestries and exotic, crafted rugs going up in flames, the very ones he'd played upon as a child. Behind the Chiens followed the men Nevina had managed to lure into her rogue forces.

Their footsteps echoed up the stone stairs as he turned to face the door. A minute later, soldiers burst through. They were far from Tumen's finest, just common hired swords who happened to stumble into the wrong part of the Fortress. Upon seeing him, they froze. Ever knew that despite their princess's assurances of his weakness, they were still afraid of the legendary blue fire. Some of them had probably seen it in battle with their own eyes. When he produced none, however, they began to hesitantly advance toward him.

His sword was much heavier than it had ever been before, even when he'd first received it as a boy, but somehow, he was able to throw his weight into the first swing. Small traces of blue flashed as he met his attackers. They came at him cautiously, one at a time at first. As he fought more and more like a man, however, instead of the legendary warrior they'd feared for so long, the soldiers became more confident. Sweat poured down Ever's temples, and his fingers trembled as he willed them to keep their grip on the sword's hilt. The world had begun to blur when a sultry voice interrupted his desperate attempt to focus.

"Well, you've certainly held your own. I didn't think you'd last this long." Nevina strolled into the tower, stepping daintily over her soldier's bodies as she made her way toward Ever. It was only as he turned to face her that he realized at least a dozen men lay at his feet, the stench of blood suddenly making the air noxious. A burning wave of dizziness set in, and Ever fell to his knees with a sickening crack on the hard stone floor. Gasping, he tried to raise himself off of all fours. Cool fingers moved gently through his hair before grabbing a fistful and yanking back so that he had to look up.

As he did, Nevina's captain walked through the door. As always, he said less than his mistress, but excitement burned brightly in his eyes. His dark cloak trailed over his men, but he didn't even attempt to avoid their corpses as the princess had. Ever tried to ready himself for his death.

They wouldn't make it easy. The princess was too ambitious, and her father had trained her well in the ways of torture. Her victory wouldn't be as rewarding if she didn't make him suffer first. The keen enthusiasm in her eyes made that clear. Despite Ever's weariness, the small smile on the captain's stone face sent a chill through him. Would they use fire? His own hearth was still lit, and the poker rested temptingly beside it. The hawks were also an option, as the balcony outside would provide ample space to watch the princess's beloved pets tear him to pieces. He also knew from the battlefield that she was particularly fond of eyes. Then there was Nevina's wicked knife, the crooked one that never left her side. But nothing he imagined prepared him for the words that came from the captain's mouth.

"The girl has arrived. She'll be up here in just a moment." Panic flooded Ever. He should have known she would try something like this. Isa was hot-tempered and stubborn. Where, he wondered, was Garin? Of all the people to get her out of the country, it should have been the steward. What had possessed him to allow her to return? Or worse yet, he thought with horror, what might have kept him from his duty? While Ever understood little about the true nature of the steward, the idea that the enemy's dark forces might have been able to thwart Garin terrified the prince more than anything.

As predicted, he could hear Isa's uneven footsteps on the stairs. He tried to call out for her to run, but Nevina jerked his head back even harder, and the captain kneed him in the chin. He was still gasping and spitting out blood when she walked in. Her eyes went wide as soon as she saw him, and they nearly glazed over when she saw his captors. As she stared, the captain walked over, grabbed her, and held her tightly. She tried to struggle, but his arms, nearly as thick as her waist, might as well have been bonds of steel. Nevina let go of Ever's hair and left him kneeling on the floor. Walking over to Isa, the princess softly tucked a stray lock of copper hair behind Isa's ear.

"Really, Everard," she murmured. "I know I was never your first choice, but you chose *this* over me?" Ever gritted his teeth as the princess lifted Isa's crooked wrist. She held it for a moment between two fingers as if it were a dead fish, then dropped it. "You've changed, my dear prince. You've grown soft. Your father at least had the good sense to see that a life with me would have been preferable to this kind of end. And what was it truly for? She lacks the strength you so desperately counted on." She walked back over to Ever and kicked him in the ribs. "Such a waste." As Ever coughed up blood, he saw a brilliant flash out of the corner of his eye.

Isa's eyes suddenly burned fiercely. A bolt of blue shot out of her right hand and traveled up the captain's arm. He let go with a cry and stumbled backward. Isa turned to run to Ever, but Nevina quickly grabbed her by the left wrist and yanked hard. Isa let out a cry of pain and the blue fire ceased as Nevina expertly twisted. The captain was quick to get up, his eyes bright with an eagerness Ever wished he could beat from the vile man's face.

"No, Your Highness," the captain said to his mistress, "I don't think there will be any waste here." Ever watched in horror as he took Isa from Nevina's arms. Nevina smiled and drew the knife from her belt.

"I've always wanted to plunge a knife into your heart," she told Ever. "Now I get to plunge one into your soul." Without pause, she buried the blade deep in Isa's chest.

Ever didn't hear his own scream. He didn't smell the smoke that was beginning to make the air in the room unbreathable. He didn't notice when a soldier stepped in to tell the princess about how the Fortress steward was making trouble downstairs. All he saw was the blood that stained Isa's dress as she lay on the floor where they'd let her fall. Slowly, he crawled over to where she lay. With a shaking hand, he tried to wipe the tears that fell ran silently down her face.

"I couldn't leave you here," she whispered.

"Hush," he gently cradled her face in his hand. Though she tried to smile at him, he could see the terror all over her face. "You have endured far too much pain at my hands to be forgivable. And yet, I must ask of you one more thing." Isa still watched him, but her eyes were beginning to look glassy. He didn't have much time left. "I simply ask you to remember me not as the monster I was, but as the man you taught to love."

"Why?" Isa whispered. "What are you saying?"

"I'm going to fix everything," he promised softly. Her eyes grew a bit wider.

"Ever, what are you doing?"

"What I should have done long ago." His hand quivered as he pulled the crystal ring from his pocket and placed it on her bloody hand. Tenderly, Ever rested his lips on her forehead as he felt the strength within him begin to bleed out.

Garin had been right. The Fortress had never abandoned him. Rather, he'd chosen to go his own way. To truly serve his people, he had to be willing to give it all and to trust that the Fortress would make it right. But the vanity of who he was and what he was had kept him from acknowledging that truth. There was only one thing in the world that could break him of that pride. His men hadn't been worth it in battle. Not even Destin had been worth it. But the Fortress had given him Isa, and Isa was worth it.

As he pushed the power from his body into hers, he could hear the bones in her wrist reset, and then in her ankle. Her breathing began to deepen again, and he knew her wound had closed. As Isa opened her eyes, they once more burned blue. Ever smiled as his own eyes closed. He felt the peace of his beloved Fortress cradle him as he welcomed death. He was willing.

CHAPTER 15

Isa had never felt such pain in her life, not when Ever's power had first touched her, not when the horse had broken her ankle or her wrist, and not even when the flaming arrows singed her skin and the bird of prey had gouged her leg. She knew immediately that the blade Princess Nevina had thrust into her chest was no ordinary blade, its dark power beginning to poison her blood as soon as it broke her skin. An icy fear seized her, and she couldn't think through the fog that suddenly clouded her vision. As the dark princess let her fall to the ground, her mind ran in circles. Ever was dying. She had seen it as he'd knelt on the floor just a few feet away.

Despair had taken her until she became faintly aware of a pleasant sensation on her face, a familiar one. The touch helped clear a way for her thoughts through the ringing in her ears. He was asking forgiveness. He was promising to make the pain go away. The seconds had seemed like eternity, but finally, she was able to open her eyes. Princess Nevina was shrieking as she ran toward them, but she stopped short. A blue cocoon of fire had encased them. Looking down, Isa realized she was gripping Ever's arm tightly with her left hand, something she'd not been able to do since she was nine.

For just a moment, she felt nothing but bliss as he softly kissed her face. His lips were still on her brow, but the longer he held on, the more she could feel him slipping away. Finally, he slumped limply to the floor. She didn't have to touch him to know that he was gone. The chill had touched his lips just as he'd let go.

"No!" Isa screamed. The blue shelter that had hidden them dissipated, and its protection with it. But that didn't matter. Isa rose slowly, and for the first time in fourteen years, stood erect. She hardly noticed though. Nevina and the man beside her watched, their mouths agape and their hands slightly raised. The agony of loss washed through Isa like a flood, and blue flames tinted her vision as anger followed the pain.

Nevina's captain made the first move. Without hesitation, Isa raised one hand, palm out. Before he could take two steps, a bolt of blue lightning threw him backwards against the wall, knocking him unconscious.

Nevina was smarter. Raising her knife, she began to walk toward Isa. Golden flames wrapped around the knife, spinning faster with each step. On instinct she didn't know she possessed, Isa knelt and slammed her fists against the floor. She could once again feel the darkness trying to ensnare her as it had on the balcony, but this time, she was ready. The power that swirled around the knife was strong, but it was no match for the power that now coursed through her. Though she'd struggled to push back against the weight of the evil strength before, Isa suddenly found it nearly effortless. The presence of the Fortress flowed around and through her, and for the first time in her life, Isa knew without a doubt what she had been born to do.

After Isa's first strike, Nevina had stumbled, but regained her balanced and continued to approach. Again, Isa pounded the floor, and this time, the blue flame flew out from her hands and traveled up to the princess's knees, making her stop momentarily. Still, she pressed on, a look of fury upon her face. When Isa struck the ground a third time, however, the flame raced up Nevina's whole body. The dark princess writhed for what seemed like an eternity before letting out a shriek of rage. Finally, she fell limp.

Isa stood there staring down at the bodies for a long time. Eventually, as the black sky began to turn gray through the wall of windows, footsteps sounded on the stone steps outside the door. A handful of the servants burst through the doors, along with a number of Chiens. They came to a halt when they saw her. It was only the expressions on their faces that made her look in the mirror. Turning to it, she realized why they seemed so terrified.

Her eyes blazed with a wild blue, as did the ring on her hand. She hadn't noticed it until now. It was the Queen's Ring. Ever must have placed it there. Looking back in the mirror, she saw a look on her face that she'd never worn before, wild and fierce. Her hair had fallen out of its place and was covered in sweat and blood, making her look even more feral. That was when, out of her peripheral vision, she realized Ever's body was gone.

"Isa," Garin finally made his way through the crowd. He approached her slowly, as if she were a wounded hound. "You're going to be alright," Isa looked up at him, suddenly terrified.

"They took him, Garin," she whispered.

"No, dear," the steward finally reached out and took her hands. Their warmth helped draw Isa back to herself. "The Fortress has taken him. He was its son, and it loved him. It will give his body a more fitting burial than we ever could." With that, Garin dropped to one knee before her, still holding the hand that wore the ring. "And now it's your burden and privilege to lead us into the next page of

Destin's future. Are you willing, Isabelle? Are you ready to be our queen?"

. . .

The Fortress's purge was finalized when the dark princess was bound, gagged, and put to death according to the law of the land. Exhausted, Isa didn't want to attend the hanging, but Garin told her it was an unfortunate duty of the monarchs to oversee the deaths of the people's enemies. Things were a little easier once that was done. By the time the sun rose, the dirt and grime were gone, and the white marble glittered in the light of the morning. The gardens bloomed with new buds, no signs of the charred dust they had been set to the night before. It was as if there had never been a battle of any kind.

Similarly, according to reports, Soudain had been purged and healed as well. The stone army had apparently returned to its human state at the same moment Ever had healed Isa. After pouring through the Fortress and finishing off Nevina's forces, they'd run down into the town and slaughtered the Caregivers as they'd attempted to escape with as many townspeople as they could find. When the sun had risen, however, all signs of bodies and blood were gone. Instead of a war-torn landscape, however, gardens and farms were suddenly filled with the ripest produce the farmers had ever seen.

Even the Chiens who had remained behind were healed and could speak again. Everything seemed not only as it should be, but better. In the days that followed, people flocked to see their new queen, the once crippled dancer who was now the most powerful ruler in the land. Isa's own family had run to her with open arms, her parents sobbing with joy, Launce bursting with pride, and little Megane as happy to see her as ever. As they held her, however, she realized their embraces still left her feeling empty. She held on to them tightly, but deep down, longed for the arms of another.

Garin and Gigi were really the only ones who understood her pain, and she realized quickly that she preferred their presence to all others'. Gigi didn't ask incessant questions like the rest of the well-meaning courtiers and servants. She would simply hold Isa, crying her own tears along with the young woman. And though he was less expressive about it, Isa could feel the pain that Garin carried with him. Human or not, he had lost a son.

The coronation ceremony was to take place a week after Ever's death. Isa relied on Garin take care of the customs and rituals she knew nothing about. She tried to smile and do as her royal tutors instructed her to, telling her when to sit, when to rise, when to speak, and when to refrain. But the emptiness inside was gnawing, and the weight of loneliness was more than she'd ever expected it to be.

The morning of the coronation, Isa snuck out of her new chambers, which had once belonged to King Rodrigue. She'd discovered quickly that her new powers allowed her to slip past people unseen if she so wished. Silently, she made her way down to the rose garden. The last time she'd sat on the stone bench had been when Ever sat beside her, just eight days before. That seemed like a different lifetime.

Everything he'd told her about the strength had begun to make sense to her. Although he'd certainly hidden much, she was beginning to understand the cryptic words and strange riddles he'd used when discussing the elusive power he possessed. When Launce had asked her about it, she'd been able to tell him little. There just weren't words for what now mixed with her lifeblood and made her heart beat.

She also understood why she hadn't been ready when Ever had asked her to marry him. She'd been trying to so hard to be ready that she'd missed the point of the strength completely. It wasn't ever hers to be begin with. It was too great to ever truly belong to a human. It was something completely other. The moment Marko had whispered that Ever was going to die, her heart had cried out. Without thinking, she'd run to the Fortress, the presence that had become her greatest comforter whenever she felt alone. Despite not being physically at the Fortress, she had somehow known it would follow her. And her cry had been answered.

"I took too long," Isa said without looking up as Garin sat down beside her. "I should have known sooner that all I had to do was ask. I could have healed him!"

"Whether you knew or not wasn't the point." For the first time in a week, Garin had shed his black garments for those more fitting of a steward welcoming his new queen. Not that Isa cared what he wore. "You might have made a mistake, but it wouldn't have mattered in the end. Our missteps aren't powerful enough to thwart the carefully laid plans of this strange place. Ever had been searching for peace for a long time, and this end was the only way he could find it."

"I wish that made it easier," Isa whispered. Garin put a hand gently on her shoulder.

"Ever would want you to rejoice for him. He gave all that was left of him to give you a life worth living. He wanted you to find joy, Isabelle." He looked up at the rising sun and tried to give her a teasing smile. "Now, if you desire to keep that life, I suggest we return you to the seamstress. She might have both our heads if your gown isn't perfect in time for the ceremony."

And before she knew it, Isa was standing outside the gigantic doors of the throne room. She attempted to stand as she'd been instructed, chin high, shoulders back, taking small steps when the horns sounded so as not to step on her flowing white and blue dress. The pearls that dangled from her ears were cold against her neck, reminders that this wasn't a dream. She'd expected to feel jittery and afraid during this ceremony, but oddly, she felt calm. This was where she was supposed to be. If only she didn't have to do it by herself.

"Presenting Her Majesty Elect, Isabelle Marchand, Chosen of the Fortress!" The throne room was brighter than she'd ever seen it, full of light and even more full of people. The draperies and chandeliers glittered with hanging diamonds that caught the light and threw it everywhere the sun didn't directly reach. As she walked slowly down the red velvet aisle, the people bowed, falling row by row. She didn't understand the strange look on their faces until she glanced down. As she walked, spiraling blue flame swirled around her faster and faster. Finally, she reached, the priest. He smiled kindly down at her, but she couldn't bring herself to smile back. He began to recite the ceremonial ordinances before taking the ring from its pillow on the short pedestal that stood between them. She had given it back the day before so that it could be properly accepted in front of the people. Garin said it was all for appearance's sake, since her true coronation had taken place when Ever had placed it on her finger.

The priest began by asking the people if they accepted her as their queen. The choral answer was loud and sure. Though Isa struggled to pay full attention to the priest's words, she had the charges memorized. He was now asking her if she was willing to accept the life of sacrifice this ring required of her.

"I am willing." None of them would be sitting there now if she wasn't. How could the priest or anyone else in the crowd truly know the sacrifice that had already taken place for her to have this position?

"Do you bond yourself forever to the Fortress and what it demands of you, relinquishing your own ambitions and designs?"

"Yes," Isa felt a tear slip down her cheek. She was glad her back was to the crowd. Before the priest could ask the next question, however, he was interrupted by the sound of the enormous doors opening once more. When Isa turned to see who had interrupted the ceremony, she nearly fell to her knees.

A man stood in the doorway. His posture was straight, and his bearing was regal. Isa began to tremble, afraid to meet his eyes. The man's hands were not misshapen, nor was his face gaunt or pale. Strong limbs were clothed in deep blue, but Isa could not bring herself to look at them for long. She stood still, frozen by the fear that she had truly lost her mind.

The crowd gasped as they recognized him, and quickly fell into an uncomfortable silence, looking back and forth between the ruler they'd just accepted and the one that should have been. Their discomfort was lost on Isa, however. Finally, she was able to meet his eyes, and when she did, she let out a cry of joy. Even from across the great room, she could see that they burned a fierce blue. She couldn't pull her own eyes away from them as he began to stride down the aisle. Before she knew what she was doing, she was sobbing, running to meet him.

He caught her in his arms and held her close. There were so many questions Isa had, but he allowed none of them. Bending down, he kissed her with a resolve that shot heat through her lips and all the way down to her fingertips and toes. Isa had never been so afraid in her life. This must be a dream. And yet, when he finally released her enough to look into her eyes, she didn't wake up. She felt her heart stumble as she reached up to touch his face. He was completely familiar, and yet, a stranger to her. He, in turn, seemed to be memorizing her features as well, a hungry look in his eyes.

"You Highness . . . Prince Everard . . . ," the priest stumbled as he tried to take back control of the ceremony. "I'm sorry, but the people have already accepted . . . ." At a loss for words, he finally looked at Isa desperately. "Your Majesty! You are now the rightful heir to the throne, and you alone. Unless, of course, you choose to marry this man." His anxiety in questioning Ever's claim to the throne was evident as he looked at the powerful man who stood before him. The crowd leaned forward, both uneasy and fascinated by the predicament. Ever simply gave her a gentle smile and touched her face with the back of his rough fingertips before dropping to one knee.

"I was going to ask you the same question," he whispered, his voice husky. "Will you marry me, Your Majesty?" Isa fought to answer with an even voice.

"With all my heart." With that, a cheer went up from the people, and the priest let out a sigh of relief. He married them then and there as they finished their vows together. The servants scurried to turn the coronation ceremony into a wedding celebration, but Isa couldn't have cared less if they'd worn sackcloths and feasted on bread and water. Her mind was full of nothing but questions. How had he come back? Where had he been all this time? How had he been healed? She didn't get to ask him, however, until it was time for the dance.

Isa's heart leapt in her chest as everyone watched her walk away from her family to meet Ever, just as the tradition demanded. Funny, she thought as she went, that her captivity in the Fortress should teach her the origins of the dance she had wanted so badly with Raoul. As they met in the middle of the crystal floor of the balcony, she curtsied.

"My lord," she murmured. "May my life strength be bound to yours."

"My lady," he took her hand and kissed it softly. "Never will I let them part." As always, the music began to play. This time was different from all the others, however. This time, Isa was wearing the silken slippers. This time, her groom swept her across the floor in a dance that felt more like flying than anything she'd ever felt in her life. Glancing at the ground, she gasped as blue flames rose around them, encircling them as they moved. She looked up at Ever in wonder. He grinned more widely in response.

"Blue is a lovely color on you, my lady," he leaned down and whispered in her ear.

"Why didn't it do this before? All those times we were dancing and I never saw it at all!"

"It was always there. You just had to see that *you* were the one the Fortress had chosen." Suddenly, the Fortress wasn't the only one that wanted her, it seemed. That hungry look returned to his eyes, and Isa couldn't deny that she felt the same desire rushing through her.

"Can we go somewhere alone, just for a few minutes?" she pleaded. A mischievous, boyish look came to Ever's face.

"With pleasure." A few minutes more and the dance was over. The priest announced that the marriage ceremony was complete, and the crowd stood to cheer for its new king and queen. Isa knew she should be thrilled and thankful, but she suddenly wanted nothing more than to simply be alone with her husband.

True to his word, once they exited the dance floor, other couples flooded it, and he led them quietly down a dark set of stairs. A few minutes later, they were seated in the rose garden. Isa opened her mouth to begin asking her questions, but before she could utter a word, his lips were pressed firmly against hers. The evening spring air was still chilly, but his strong hands, now ungloved, kept her warm as they gently explored her face, then her neck. Her breathing hitched as they found their way to her waist and the small of her back. She could feel his desire as he drew her even closer. Isa fought to get control of her thoughts, knowing that if she gave him just half a minute more, her chance to ask would be gone for the rest of the evening.

She had to push his shoulders back with quite a bit of force before he realized she wanted to stop. She laughed a bit at his confused expression as she drew back.

"I just need to know . . . How are you here?" she gazed at him in wonder, tracing the contour of his brow with her finger. "You gave me all your strength. How did you survive?" Suddenly, she felt ridiculously as if she might begin to cry, although she wasn't sure why. Understanding lit his face as he took her left hand. Before answering, he gently explored her wrist where it had once been broken.

"When I was little, I never wondered at the wisdom this place exuded. It brought me peace, and that was enough. As I grew, however, and followed in my father's footsteps, I forgot the truth I'd known since I was born. I deluded myself into believing the strength was mine, that I was responsible for it all. I didn't realize that such a responsibility is a burden far too great for any man to bear." His face now solemn, he looked into Isa's eyes, and for a moment, she saw the sadness in them that had haunted him for so long.

"And you. What I did to you as a boy was more than I knew how to endure. Garin told me that I could be forgiven, but my father made it very clear that I was never to go near you again. I could have done the right thing at any time, but my pride was too great. I simply couldn't stand to look at what I'd done, and as a result, you haunted both my dreams and my waking moments. By the time you returned to me, I was so desperate to hold on to my dwindling power that I was too much of a selfish coward to give it to you." He paused and took a deep breath.

"I spent so many hours, so many days and nights trying to come up with ways to break the curse. I sought every action known to man to redeem myself and my home, and yet, in the end it was nothing I did that broke the curse." Isa was confused.

"You healed me. Wasn't that when the curse was broken?"

"Yes, but it wasn't my action that broke the curse. Rather, it was my heart." Isa shook her head.

"I still don't understand."

"A new strength had to be found. You, Isa, brought a strength back to the Fortress that I'd once known as a child. Your strength wasn't military might or skill with a sword. You brought the power of the heart. You taught me once again how much strength lies in love.

"Second, what was broken had to be remade. Yes, I had broken you as a child. I, myself, had been broken in body, but even more importantly, I had been broken in spirit long before that. I had to have my trust in the Fortress, my relationship with it healed. Truths I'd abandoned as a young man needed to be made real to me again. At the moment I happily gave of myself, I, too, was healed.

"Finally, I had to be willing to die. This was the hardest one for me to understand. I thought I had been willing to die before, but what I risked in battle was no true risk. I grew up on the battlefield where men die every day, but my strength allowed me to desperately cling to life. With it, I could never truly know what it means to sacrifice for my kingdom, or even for you. The Fortress knew that for me to truly serve my people, I needed to understand self-sacrifice. The only way I could learn that was for the Fortress to loosen my vice grip on my power."

Suddenly, Ever's breath shook as he spoke his next words. "Isa, the moment I thought she had killed you, my world lost its meaning. I realized I had no reason to hang onto my power if it meant living without you. You had brought light into my darkness. You were the only reason I was ever able to truly hope, and if you died, it would be because of my selfish ambition. Giving you the rest of my strength was the easiest thing I've ever done. I was more than willing to die. And in offering up my strength, I found a peace. I could die serenely, knowing once again that I was forgiven and that I was loved." With that, Ever stood and Isa stood with him. He'd leaned in for another kiss when they were interrupted by the sound of a clearing throat.

"What is it Garin?" Ever nearly growled, and Isa giggled.

"I apologize, Sire, but the people are beginning to wonder where you are. It's nearly time for the final ceremony."

"We'll be there in a few minutes," Ever snapped. Isa laughed again. His temper hadn't changed as much as his appearance, and it put her at ease to see so much of the old prince in the body of the intimidating new king.

"It's strange how the things that brought you peace and healed you were the same things that helped me as well," Isa said. "And yet, we were broken so differently. I always blamed my weakness for being the reason I was unusable. And yet, it was my very weakness that allowed me to fulfill my role here." She gave a dry laugh. "If I'd been whole, if I'd never been injured, I would be a dancer now, married to Raoul." She shook her head. Compared to what she had now, that existence was the last thing she could ever desire, the wisp of a future she never wanted to consider again.

"This place has a strange way of working things out like that." They both looked up in wonder at the soaring white towers above them that glistened even in the dark.

"One more thing I don't understand," she said as they slowly walked back. "Why did you just disappear? Why did it take a whole week for you to return?"

"I'm not certain, but I have an idea." He gave her a sideways glance. "If I'd been there after Nevina was defeated, would you have seen yourself as queen?"

"I'm not sure," Isa shrugged. "I suppose not. I probably would have looked to you for direction."

"Exactly. Without me, you had to admit to yourself, the Fortress, and the people that this was truly your place. You were *meant* to be queen, with or without me." Isa nodded as she thought about this. As she did, another question popped into her head.

"Where were you though?" Ever chuckled a bit before answering.

"I'm not really sure. The Fortress brought me to a place of healing and dreams. I have to admit that it was a relief. I haven't had a tranquil dream since I was quite young."

"What did you dream about for an entire week?"

"Some dreams were memories. Others were scenes of a life I'd never lived, a life of peace and children and gray hair." Ever laughed a bit. "I can't recall many of them, but I do remember one thing in particular."

"What was that?" Isa found herself breathless as she awaited his reply. In response, he stopped walking, drew her to him, and leaned down to kiss her again.

"You."

ABOUT THE AUTHOR

Brittany Fichter writes about neurological disorders, education, and faith on her website, *BrittanyFichterWrites.com*. She's had articles published in magazines such as *The Old Schoolhouse, Kids' Ark Magazine,* and *The Autism Notebook*. Brittany earned her Bachelor of Science in Elementary Education from the University of Nevada, Las Vegas.

As Brittany grew up with Tourette Syndrome, Obsessive-Compulsive tendencies, and chronic anxiety, reading fantasy helped her to better understand her daily struggles. Stories of underdog heroes defeating powerful villains inspired her when her world was full of angst. As a result, she writes her own stories to reflect how the pieces of us that seem broken are what God uses to fulfill His ultimate purposes in us.

Brittany is a Las Vegas native, but she lives with her husband, daughter, and spoiled black Labrador wherever the Air Force has most recently placed them. When she's not writing, she loves reading, dancing, decorating cakes, organizing, and belting Disney princess songs at the top of her lungs. She's currently working on more fairy tale retellings, three memoirs, an original fantasy trilogy, and whatever else piques her interest.

Connect with Me:

Follow me on Twitter:@BFichterWrites
Find me on Facebook: Facebook.com/brittanyfichterwrites
Subscribe to my blog: BrittanyFichterWrites.com
Email me: BrittanyFichterWrites@gmail.com

39798669R10133

Made in the USA
Lexington, KY
12 March 2015